CATALOGUE OF AN EXHIBITION HELD IN

THE KING'S LIBRARY

BRITISH LIBRARY REFERENCE DIVISION

9 AUGUST – 22 OCTOBER

1978

A Giovanni Mardersteig
con ammirazione e amichevolmente
Pietro Annigoni

THE OFFICINA BODONI

MONTAGNOLA · VERONA

BOOKS PRINTED BY

GIOVANNI MARDERSTEIG

ON THE HAND PRESS

1923–1977

JOHN BARR

PUBLISHED FOR

THE BRITISH LIBRARY

© 1978, The British Library Board

ISBN 0 7141 0398 5 *paper*

ISBN 0 7141 0399 3 *cased*

Published by British Museum Publications Ltd, 6 Bedford Square, London WC1B 3RA

 British Library Cataloguing in Publication Data

Barr, John, b.1934
   The Officina Bodoni.
     1. Mardersteig, Giovanni
     2. Printing – Exhibitions
     I. Title   II. British Library. Reference Division
      016.094   Z232.M/

Frontispiece: Giovanni Mardersteig. Portrait sketch by Pietro Annigoni, 1954

Designed by Sebastian Carter

Set in 'Monotype' Dante and printed in Great Britain at The Curwen Press, Plaistow, London

ACKNOWLEDGEMENTS

The British Library Board would like to thank the following who have generously lent to this exhibition:

Mr Tony Appleton
Mr David Chambers
Signor Martino Mardersteig
Mr John Ryder
Mr and Mrs Hans Schmoller
The Curators of the Bodleian Library, Oxford
The Department of Prints & Drawings, British Museum, London
The Syndics of the Cambridge University Library.

Photographs of Officina Bodoni productions are also reproduced by kind permission.

The Board wishes to express to Signor Martino Mardersteig, to Mr John Ryder and to Mr and Mrs Hans Schmoller its deep appreciation of the advice and assistance they have given in planning the exhibition. They would like in particular to thank Signor Mardersteig for making available the draft of the definitive bibliography of the Officina Bodoni's work, with an introduction by Hans Schmoller, to be published later this year in a German edition by the Maximilian-Gesellschaft, Hamburg: Giovanni Mardersteig, *Die Officina Bodoni. Das Werk einer Handpresse, 1923–1977*. An English version will be issued in this country by The Bodley Head: *The Officina Bodoni. An account of the work of a hand press, 1923–1977*.

Permission to quote from the following sources is gratefully acknowledged:

John Dreyfus: 'Giovanni Mardersteig' in *The Book Club of California Quarterly News-Letter*, vol. 37 no. 2 1971.

— *On the work of Giovanni Mardersteig with 'Monotype' faces*. Monotype, 1957.

Hermann Hesse: 'Die Officina Bodoni in Montagnola', in *Neue Zürcher Zeitung*, Feuilleton, 4 November 1923.

Giovanni Mardersteig: *Ein Leben den Büchern gewidmet*, Mainz 1968. (An address given on the occasion of the first award of the Gutenberg Prize by the City of Mainz and the Gutenberg-Gesellschaft, 23 June 1968.)

John Ryder: 'Scholar–printer–publisher at Verona', in *Scholarly Publishing*, October 1971.

— 'The Officina Bodoni', in *Librarium* (Review of the Swiss Society of Bibliophiles), vol. 14 no. ii 1971.

— 'The Officina Bodoni', *The Private Library*, vol. 5 no. 4 Winter 1972.

Hans Schmoller: 'A gentleman of Verona', in *The Penrose Annual*, 1958.

ZENO C. 16 e 14

—

IN PRINCIPIO ERA IL
VERBO, E IL VERBO ERA
PRESSO DIO, ED ERA
DIO IL VERBO.

In principio era il Verbo, e il
Verbo era presso Dio, ed era
Dio il Verbo. Era questi in principio presso Dio. Le cose tutte
furono fatte per mezzo di lui, e
senza di lui nulla fu fatto
di quanto esiste.

IN PRINCIPIO ERA IL VERBO,
E IL VERBO ERA PRESSO DIO,
ED ERA DIO IL VERBO.

Specimen of Zeno type specially reset for *Librarium* (1971).

FOREWORD

In the present exhibition the British Library's own holdings of Officina Bodoni books are shown, supplemented by extensive loans from private collections and from other institutions in this country. Dr Mardersteig was an old friend and munificent benefactor of the Library. A considerable number of important exhibits were presented to the Library by the printer when they were published. The exhibition is intended, therefore, not only to honour the memory of a great scholar-printer but also to express our thanks and to demonstrate in some measure the Officina Bodoni's close and continuous connection with the literature, printing and publishing of the English-speaking world. Other exhibitions abroad will select from the productions of half a century so as to deal more thoroughly with the Officina Bodoni's relations with the cultures of Mardersteig's native Germany and his adopted homeland, Italy.

It has not been our aim in this exhibition to show a copy of every book ever printed on the hand presses of the Officina Bodoni, something which would now be difficult to do even in Verona. The loans generously placed at our disposal, however, have enabled us to exhibit more than one copy of especially important or beautiful books, and to suggest what is distinctive and sometimes unprecedented in the work of the Officina Bodoni.

Catalogue entries for Officina Bodoni books include notes on the particular copies exhibited. Here it has been considered useful to include brief descriptions of bindings originating in the Officina Bodoni, although in most cases limitations of space have precluded the showing of bindings.

For convenience the imprint 'Editiones Officinae Bodoni' is given for books of which the Officina Bodoni was the publisher, although these words do not always occur in the book. The page measurements are given, height before width, to the nearest 5 mm, to allow for the slight variations in the dimensions of hand-made and mould-made papers. Descriptions of paper taken from previous catalogues, from colophons and from the draft of the forthcoming bibliography are not in all cases conclusive; the German language does not make the distinction between mould-made and hand-made papers, which only a study of the watermarks and the Officina's records will eventually settle.

In 1954 Mardersteig was persuaded to exhibit in the Plantin-Moretus Museum, Antwerp, books printed on the hand press; the exhibition was shown in the King's Library, the British Museum, in the same year, and subsequently Officina Bodoni exhibitions have been seen in ten European cities. The original catalogue, *Officina Bodoni, Verona: catalogue of books printed on the hand press, 1923–54*, has accordingly been updated for printing in several languages. The 1954 editions contain 104 titles, the 1962 (Italian) edition 117 titles, the 1964 (Dutch) and the 1965 (French) edition 124 titles. In 1968 a supplementary catalogue was issued in Italian listing the titles from no. 101 to no. 145. These extensions and revisions have in some instances resulted in confusion in the numbering. In this exhibition catalogue, therefore, reference has been made (in round brackets) to the 1954 English catalogue for books published up to that date; for later books the number from the Italian supplementary catalogue (1968) is quoted, where applicable, in bold type. In the forthcoming definitive bibliography the numbering will be completely revised.

Quotations in Mardersteig's own words are, unless otherwise stated, from *Ein Leben den Büchern gewidmet* (1968).

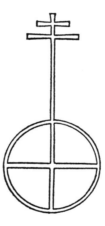

Device on a votive tablet, dated 1402, in the cathedral at Modena.

CATALOGUE

Introduction

This exhibition of books printed on the hand press of the Officina Bodoni is a memorial tribute to its founder, Dr Giovanni Mardersteig, who died on 27 December 1977, a few days before his 86th birthday.

Mardersteig set up his hand press in 1922 in Montagnola di Lugano, Switzerland, and on it he printed his first books with types cast, by special permission, from the original matrices of the great Italian printer and letter-cutter Giambattista Bodoni held in the Museo Bodoniano at Parma. From this privilege the press derived its name. In 1927, the Officina Bodoni was entrusted with the design and printing of the national edition of the works of the Italian poet Gabriele D'Annunzio. The hand press was accordingly removed from Switzerland to Verona, where it has remained ever since.

On the completion of the D'Annunzio edition in 49 volumes the Officina Bodoni widened the scope of its activities. The acquisition of lithographic and copper-plate presses made possible the production of books illustrated by modern artists. The repertoire of types was expanded to include other type faces besides those of Bodoni, and eventually some designed by Mardersteig himself and cut under his supervision.

The hand press has printed a total of nearly two hundred separate books, the greater part of which are to be seen in the exhibition. These books have all been produced to exacting editorial and scholarly standards, with carefully chosen materials and following Mardersteig's designs, at every stage under his close supervision. They are all printed with an exceptional precision, clarity and elegance because Mardersteig was, as Will Carter, himself a distinguished English printer, said, 'probably the finest pressman the world has ever seen or is ever likely to see'.

After the Second World War Mardersteig established the Stamperia Valdonega alongside the Officina Bodoni, in order to make available to a wider public finely printed books in larger editions than was possible on the hand press. The machine-set and machine-printed books of the Stamperia Valdonega are now produced under the direction of his son, Martino.

This is the second exhibition of Officina Bodoni books to be held in the King's Library. In 1954 the Department of Printed Books mounted a loan exhibition of every book printed up to that time on the hand press. It was the first exhibition in this gallery to be devoted to the work of a contemporary artist or writer during his life.

In his preface to the catalogue the great typographer and historian of printing, Stanley Morison, recalled first that Mardersteig 'has for thirty years acted on the

The printer and the book-binder. Engravings by Jost Amman (1568).

belief that to confer fine typographical form upon a fine piece of literature is a justifiable use of time and labour, material and skill; secondly that no quality of impression, however fine, can excuse inattention to textual precision. Upwards of a hundred works of literature, scrupulously chosen (in many instances critically edited by himself) . . . attest their printer's title to enduring fame'.

In his 1954 preface Morison also maintained that the historical importance of the invention of printing, which made it a powerful new intellectual instrument, lay in the possibility of multiplying a text:

'The grand achievement of the engraver, the type founder, compositor and pressman was to create the mechanical basis for standards of strict authenticity and literal exactitude . . . Multiplication in quantity and with invariability of an author's or designer's intention was at last effected'.

What, then, is the value of a private press in the modern world? Is it simply a producer of books of which the prices have been artificially inflated by a limitation of the number of copies printed – a negation of the very nature of printing? The size of the Officina Bodoni's editions, however, is determined by the use of the hand press. Why, then, use an obsolete method when modern machinery can produce more copies more quickly? The quality of the work produced on the hand press of the Officina Bodoni is its ultimate justification.

Morison stated that Mardersteig's place in the history of printing as both an artist-printer and a scholar-publisher 'cannot be far from singular and is possibly unique'. What does this mean?

Mardersteig believed that printing on the hand press encourages in the printer the strictest attention to detail and makes possible the greatest subtlety in impression. For him the hand press was like an artist's pencil, under the direct control of the printer's hand and eye, enabling immediate and direct expression of his conceptions and designs. Only he who has printed with the hand press and accustomed his eye to its slow progress can appreciate the importance of every detail. From this point of view even the most perfect machine can never replace the hand press.

Mardersteig's insistence on the importance of the craftsman's hand and eye played a decisive part in his own type designs, most of which were cut by the hand of a highly skilled punch-cutter. He similarly insisted upon using modern engravers to reinterpret and recut early woodcut designs for his Officina Bodoni books, so that type and illustration were perfectly matched in quality of craftsmanship. To the reader, the collector and the visitor to this exhibition it is evident that when Mardersteig set out to do something supremely well, hand composition and the hand press provided him with the means to do it.

How did Mardersteig see the printer's task? In *Ein Leben den Büchern gewidmet* he defined it like this:

First, service to the author, searching for the form best suited to his subject.

Second, service to the reader, making reading as pleasant and easy for him as possible.

Third, giving an attractive appearance to the whole book without imposing too much of his own personality or idiosyncrasies.

The books in this exhibition, set by hand and printed by hand are not the rivals of good machine composition and printing, nor do they offer an elegant but anachronistic substitute for the modern processes. They are something different. Rather have these editions served as an example and inspiration for fine printing carried out by modern methods, in particular for that of the Stamperia Valdonega, founded and operated by Mardersteig himself and which still works to the high standards set by experience on the hand press. 'We believe that our intimate experience with the hand press has been much to the advantage of our machine printing', Mardersteig wrote as early as 1929. Machine printing, which Mardersteig had hitherto done only in isolated instances, became in 1948 an integral part of his work. It is generally agreed that the Stamperia Valdonega has exerted a powerful influence on book printing in Italy, and in recognition of this in 1962 the Italian government awarded Mardersteig the gold medal for 'Benemeriti della cultura'. (After the Second World War Mardersteig became an Italian citizen and assumed the name Giovanni.)

The citation reads:

'Gabriele D'Annunzio has justly called him "Prince of Printers". Giovanni Mardersteig has in his long career reached the heights of the arts of printing and of the book, upon which, as the creator of new types and of splendid editions, he leaves the deep trace of his genius. His example in the fields of typography and publishing has both a national and universal importance because it reminds us that printing is an art before it is an industry'.

The block-cutter and the type-caster. Engravings by Jost Amman (1568).

Type-cutting and type-founding

The process of founding hot-metal type is fundamentally the same whether it is done by hand or by machine. A steel punch, on the end of which the letter is engraved in relief, is struck into a piece of a softer metal alloy to produce a hollow matrix, into which the molten type-metal is poured. When punches are cut by hand in the traditional manner the punch-cutter, following an enlarged drawing of the letter (of which in some instances he is also the designer), engraves the letter on to the punch in the actual size of the type to be produced.

All punches were cut by hand until the invention in 1885 of the punch-cutting machine, by which a pantograph traces the outline of a large drawn letter and automatically cuts a letter scaled down to the required reduction. Machine engraving uses a series of diminutive routers following the contours of the pattern in relief, and allows the type-designer to dispense with the craft of the engraver or punch-cutter.

In the past some of the finest type faces were cut by engravers who were also masters of printing techniques. Nicolas Jenson in the fifteenth century and Giambattista Bodoni in the eighteenth used type faces that reflect a unity of design and production only possible in a small organization, and no longer commercially practicable in twentieth-century conditions. Nevertheless, Mardersteig was in our own age just such a type-designer. His Dante type face, moreover, designed for use in the limited editions of the hand press, was acquired and released for general use by the Monotype Corporation.

A hand letter-cutter unconsciously modifies a design according to whether he cuts it large or small, aiming primarily at legibility in small sizes and at good looks in the large ones. When working in modern industrial conditions a type-designer has to provide carefully for these modifications which would be made without thinking by a good punch-cutter.

Type-setting

For four centuries after the invention of printing type was set ('composed') by hand by a compositor who selected from the case of types the letters he needed for the text. This process required considerable quantities of pre-cast type.

The invention of the type-casting machine then made possible supplies of type in sufficient quantities for type-setting to be performed mechanically and much faster. Hot-metal composing machines could then be developed, including the Monotype patented by Tolbert Lanston in 1887. The Monotype system uses matrices arranged in a grid from which the caster selects the letters to be presented to the mould (fed with molten type-metal from below) so as to cast single types in justified lines. The caster is controlled by a paper ribbon previously perforated on a separate keyboard.

Giovanni Mardersteig: early years

Hans Mardersteig, the son of a lawyer, was born on 8 January 1892 in Weimar. His paternal grandfather, a well-known history painter, had in his youth known Goethe; his maternal grandfather was the sculptor Gustav Bläser, whose works are to be found on both sides of the Atlantic. The grand ducal court of Weimar had since Goethe's day continued as a notable centre for the arts. Men such as the architect Henri van de Velde worked in Weimar; Count Harry Kessler, who set up his Cranach Press on the model of the private presses in England, was one of the many distinguished visitors to the Mardersteig home.

Mardersteig's education was calculated to develop both his intellectual and manual abilities; with his three brothers, he was encouraged to use his hands by spending some time working with carpenters, printers and other skilled craftsmen. He studied law and art history at the universities of Bonn, Vienna, Kiel and Jena. His doctoral thesis in law was accepted in 1915 but his real interest was in art.

Mardersteig suffered from tuberculosis and was unfit for military service. He spent the early years of the First World War in legal administration in Germany, but his health obliged him in 1916 to move to Switzerland. In 1917 there was an exhibition of modern German painting in the Kunsthaus in Zürich in which an important section was devoted to the Expressionists. Mardersteig organised this section, which was a great success.

'Genius'

Mardersteig and his friend Carl Georg Heise made plans for a new art periodical. These they submitted to Kurt Wolff, a publisher with an enterprising list of modern authors, together with detailed proposals on how his list could be extended into the field of art, suggesting subjects and suitable authors. Wolff too was an art lover only slightly older than Mardersteig and Heise, and was convinced by their plans.

In 1919 the first of six issues of *Genius* came out, edited by Mardersteig, Heise and (at Wolff's instigation) the young literary critic, Kurt Pinthus. A number of notable artists, critics and art historians became contributors so that *Genius* reflected and interpreted German art and culture during the troubled but exciting post-war period. *Genius* only ceased publication because Mardersteig's health compelled him to retreat to Switzerland and Heise took up a museum post in Lübeck. Both men remained advisers and close friends of Wolff's.

1

Genius.   Zeitschrift für werdende und alte Kunst.
Edited by Carl Georg Heise, Hans Mardersteig and Kurt Pinthus.
Printed by W. Drugulin, Leipzig. The device designed by Emil Preetorius.
Kurt Wolff Verlag: Leipzig, 1919.   P.P.1931.ddf.

The prospectus explained the aims of the new journal: 'The painting, sculpture, architecture and the applied arts of all ages, especially our own, will be presented and elucidated through carefully chosen illustrations in large format and through original graphics'. It continued: 'The past will not be treated with antiquarian curiosity but as something living, brought through selection and interpretation into a fruitful relationship with the present'.

Mardersteig was responsible for the design of *Genius*, for its layout and production. He supervised the colour reproductions and saw it through the press during the three years it was published.

Printing and the hand press

Mardersteig's experience with *Genius* led him to the conclusion that the highest achievements in book production could only be reached when the editing, design, printing and binding were controlled and closely supervised by a single individual.

At the end of the First World War there was a shortage of good materials; paper, printing inks, bindings were generally poor. 'Among my fellow-workers in the publishing house in Leipzig', Mardersteig recalls, 'there was a man who shared my predilection for good quality and with whom I made endless trips to printers and bookbinders . . . This man, a bookbinder named Demeter, had worked in England for T. J. Cobden-Sanderson. My interest in Cobden-Sanderson's Doves Press was further nourished, for his editions seemed to me to surpass, through the simplicity and quality of the printing and the type, the books of William Morris, Charles Ricketts or even St. John Hornby'.

Mardersteig's dissatisfaction with the standards of work done under his supervision by others, together with the example of the English private presses, led him to consider founding a hand press of his own. 'When . . . a chronic illness forced me to leave the harsh climate of Munich and exchange this for a life in the south . . . at Montagnola near Lugano, faithful Demeter with youthful energy and devotion helped me in the first difficult months to set up the press'.

The Bodoni types

'What characterizes the productions of a hand press is in the first place . . . the type. In my case the type gave its name to the press: Officina Bodoni. It was by accident that I had discovered the incomparable punch-cutter Giambattista Bodoni, who left us more than four hundred types and enjoyed a great reputation as printer to the Dukes of Parma. When I was a student on a journey through Italy I was browsing through the books at an antiquarian bookseller's and came across a Bodoni edition in quarto of 1811. The title at first made me smile – *Périclès: de l'Influence des Beaux Arts sur la Félicité Publique par Charles D'Alberg*'. Mardersteig was impressed by the beauty of the type, the perfection of the printing and the elegance of the format of this book. 'The extraordinarily clear impression of the type, its uniformity and deep black colour, its pages with the type area framed with wide margins, as fresh as if it had been printed yesterday on magnificent handmade paper – all this remained in my mind, although at the time I certainly had no typographical aspirations'.

'While I was still in Germany, pondering my future work with the hand press and the choice of literary texts, I was always stuck when it came to the question of where I should get my type . . . To have a type cut for me would have been too expensive and too time-consuming, and above all, I was not yet experienced enough to choose the right letter forms'. The types used by the English private presses seemed to him anachronistic and consciously archaic. Mardersteig admits that Bodoni was equally out of date. 'And yet I repeatedly returned to his types, which I got to know rather well having made a small collection of his books'. In a Leipzig printing house Mardersteig came across the Walbaum types, already familiar to him from his grand-father's library, for Walbaum had lived in Weimar and obviously supplied the surrounding printing houses with his types. 'My discovery that Walbaum originally stemmed from Bodoni . . . strengthened my conviction that it would be best to reach back to Bodoni and choose his type for my future press. A good recutting did not at that time exist'.

In Rome Mardersteig met a young Italian equally interested in Bodoni and together they obtained permission from the Italian government to cast types from Bodoni's original matrices which survive in the museum at Parma.

Giambattista Bodoni (1740–1813)

Towards the end of the eighteenth century certain printers, such as Didot in France and Bodoni in Italy, adopted an austere typographical style which has since been called neo-classical, though it is far from a direct revival of the letter-forms of the ancient world. Their types, still known as 'Modern face', mark the extreme stage of a development which began earlier in the century, a movement away from letter-forms based on handwriting towards types that are heavily modelled, i.e. with an abrupt contrast between thick and thin strokes. Giambattista Bodoni, who was director of the ducal printing house at Parma from 1768, designed and cut such types. With them he printed luxurious editions which are famous for the imposing sobriety of their layout. Bodoni made sparing use of ornament and illustration, but even in a small format his unerring skill in arranging text on a page enabled him to achieve a monumental effect.

2

Jean-François Momoro: *Le Traité élémentaire de l'imprimerie.*
Paris, 1793.

Mardersteig had no formal training as a printer beyond a few months' voluntary 'apprenticeship' in the Officina Serpentis in Steglitz. The types, methods and style of this press were not to his taste. 'My real guide to the hand press was an old French text book, *Le Traité élémentaire de l'imprimerie*'.

Mardersteig mentions one of the reasons for his life-long enthusiasm for his chosen medium: 'The great advantage of a hand press is the fact that the slow process permits printing on damp hand-made paper. The ink is more easily received by a paper made of rags and hemp which has become flexible through wetting. Considerably less ink is required than in dry-printing and a sharper and more even impression is obtained'. Mardersteig was then, as he was for many years, his own press-man. 'The constant delight of the printer in his work is the fresh appearance of flawless matt black on the damp paper'.

The first Officina Bodoni books

From the enormous range of Bodoni's types Mardersteig first chose a few founts belonging to Bodoni's later typographic style, and in particular 16-point 'Catania', 20-point 'Casale' and 12-point 'Cuneo' as well as a decorated italic. With this restricted range of characters he printed texts of different kinds: verse, plays, and prose. 'Right from the start books produced by the Officina Bodoni were of impeccable quality – there were no preliminary falterings', John Dreyfus observed. The prevailing severity of Bodoni's original style was sometimes tempered by a deliberate choice of Bodoni's more ornamental types and by decoration on the bindings.

3

NIETZSCHE · ZWEI REDEN ZARATHUSTRAS

A trial proof set in 16-point Bodoni roman. 12 copies. 12 pages. 27.5×20 cm.
Officina Bodoni: Montagnola, January 1923.   Loan

Before the first books of the Officina Bodoni were issued four trial proofs were made
in small editions, of which this is the second.

VON DEN BEIDEN ABSCHNITTEN AUS NIETZSCHES
ZARATHUSTRA WURDEN IM JANUAR 1923 ZWŒLF
DRUCKE HERGESTELLT ALS ZWEITE PROBE DER
OFFICINA BODONI IN MONTAGNOLA

4

ANGELO POLIZIANO · ORPHEI TRAGEDIA

Italian text of the dramatic poem written in 1471.
A trial proof of the first book published by the Officina Bodoni in April 1923.
20 copies on mould-made paper.
Set in Bodoni 16-point roman and italic. 28 pages. 30×20 cm.
Officina Bodoni: Montagnola, February 1923. (1)
Marbled paper boards.   Loan

The earliest dramatic poem in Italian, on the story of Orpheus and Eurydice, was written in 1471 by the Florentine humanist Poliziano when he was seventeen years old. It was commissioned by Cardinal Francesco Gonzaga for the festivities which marked a double wedding at the ducal court of Mantua.

The first important book with which Giambattista Bodoni began his career at Parma in 1769 was also in celebration of a marriage, that of his patron, the Duke of Parma. On this occasion Gluck's opera *Orfeo ed Euridice* was performed for the first time in Italy, the libretto of which is based on Poliziano's dramatic poem. Bodoni later published an edition of Poliziano's sonnets, but not of the *Orfeo*.

'How easy everything seems as one plans it in hopeful innocence, and how hard is harsh reality and practical experience', wrote Mardersteig. The first proof sheets from the press, Goethe's *Urworte Orphisch*, set in the newly cast Bodoni 16-point roman type had been marred by a black dot in the counter of the lower case e, caused by a defect in the casting. On dry-printing the e was perfect, but Mardersteig, following Baskerville and later masters, printed his books on moistened paper. In printing the damp paper was pushed into the type and picked up this defect which appeared on the page as a small black dot.

'On account of this experience I did not dare start printing my first book even though the fine hand-made paper from the house of Marais in France had already arrived. Instead of pulling trial proofs I printed the entire text on ordinary sheets of another kind of paper . . . one of the charming poems by the young Poliziano, the greatest master of the Italian language after Petrarch. The final printing in fifty copies was accomplished without trouble'.

The extraordinary care, patience and perfectionism which Mardersteig always brought to his task were thus apparent from the start.

5

MICHELAGNIOLO BUONARROTI · POESIE

Italian text; 21 sonnets, 3 epigrams and 76 madrigals.
A selection of a hundred poems made by Michelangelo during his lifetime and prepared for printing, but hitherto unpublished in this form and here reassembled from the manuscripts.
5 copies on vellum and 175 on mould-made Marais paper.
Set in 16-point Bodoni roman and italic. 124 pages. 28.5×20 cm.
Editiones Officinae Bodoni: Montagnola, July 1923. (2)
Vellum boards, solid device on upper cover, black leather label on spine.　　　Loan

Mardersteig recalled that in the printing of this edition of Michelangelo's poems another difficulty had to be overcome. Marks in the hand-made paper, caused by rusty equipment in the paper mill, led to weeks of delay, until a fresh supply of paper could be obtained.

6

PERCY BYSSHE SHELLEY · EPIPSYCHIDION

English text of the poem published anonymously in 1821 while Shelley was living
in Pisa.
222 copies printed in black and blue on mould-made Marais paper.
Set in 16-point Bodoni roman and italic. 40 pages. 28.5×20 cm.
Editiones Officinae Bodoni: Montagnola, November 1923. (4)
Vellum boards, solid device on upper cover.   Cup.510.ee.1

The Officina Bodoni in Montagnola

The novelist Hermann Hesse, a friend and neighbour of Mardersteig's, wrote a short
but perceptive article on the Officina Bodoni which appeared in the *Neue Zürcher
Zeitung* Feuilleton, 4 November 1923. Although only four books had been printed,
Hesse was able to put his finger on the press's distinctive excellence in remarks which
remain applicable to its whole *oeuvre*. The article was shortly afterwards reprinted
as a booklet by the publisher Jakob Hegner.

'As long as civilization exists there will always be a few people with a taste for luxury
not only in the usual objects of fashion but also in books. For every one of their
number, certainly, there are hundreds of wealthy men who would never wear a
ready-made suit or cheap machine-made shoes, but who, when it comes to books,
cannot recognise the difference between factory and hand production. However, to
the few who are discriminating in this respect and have learnt to use their eyes, there
is as great a difference between a book printed in the conventional way and one carefully produced by hand, as there is between a type-written business letter and the
lovingly written manuscript of a monastic calligrapher.

'These connoisseurs of book production will be delighted to hear that a new book
press was set up a few months ago where work of the highest quality is being done.
This is the Officina Bodoni in Montagnola di Lugano. Its first publications are now
before us: so far, four extraordinarily fine and carefully produced pieces ...

'Of the texts from this press we will say no more than that they all demonstrate
great care and connoisseurship in their selection and editing. The real importance of
their production lies not in this editorial skill but in the printing by hand. On that
score, may I say a few words as a book lover and as a neighbour and occasional eye-
witness of the work at Montagnola. The printing is done by the director of the new
press, with three or four assistants, and the books are put together in the house, with
the exception of certain parts of the binding, e.g. the gilding. That which in a big

mechanized printing house would take merely hours and days here requires weeks and months of painstaking work by craftsmen.

'The type-setting of each page is the subject of long consultations and numerous trials. In such printing there is not a comma, page number, initial nor even a space which is not the result of devoted labour, patient experiment and a cultivated judgement. The setting is finished, proofs are read and re-read with scrupulous attention to detail and then comes the delicate business of printing. The paper – of course, only of the best quality – is carefully checked sheet by sheet. It is slightly moistened and a first trial proof is pulled for which the minimum pressure is exerted. This trial proof may appear perfectly adequate to the layman – there are no obvious mistakes, no more imperfections than you would come across in the normal run of books. Here, however, each slight fluctuation, every variation in the strength and intensity of the print is very closely examined.

'Hours are spent on the thorough checking of every single sheet before the final printing. By inserting an underlay of tissue paper, doubled, tripled or quadrupled in the required places, an impression is obtained in which all unevenness, faintness or irregularity of impression have been eliminated. Once you realise that the same rigorous attention to detail is applied in all processes down to the finishing of the bound volume, then you have some idea of the quality of this handcraft operation. Books of this sort are a far cry from mass-produced commodities; each single impression is the result of discriminating judgment and highly skilled workmanship. Naturally, the editions are small, seldom more than two hundred copies, and the prices are high. Nevertheless, the handsome, vellum-bound volume of Michelangelo, for instance, at 120 francs, which would have taken several men some months to produce, is not expensive in relation to the work involved'.

Hesse explains why the press is called the Officina Bodoni: 'The name is that of one of the greatest printers of all time, Giambattista Bodoni, who worked in Parma towards the end of the eighteenth century . . . He originated in modern times the concept of the book as a work of art, that is, the book which owes its beauty not to its decoration, illustrations, binding or display of gold, but purely to the dignity and charm of its perfect hand production. The new press calls itself after the splendid Bodoni, not as a compliment to him or as a way of attracting honour to itself, but for the following very good reason:

The Officina Bodoni has in fact received from the Italian government the sole right to use the original letters of Bodoni – the matrices, that is, the moulds of his different alphabets, which have been kept in the museum at Parma and from which for the first time in a hundred years types have again been cast . . .' Hesse compares favourably the use made of the types by the new press with Bodoni's own books, which 'can radiate a strength and confidence that recalls the brilliant, concise clarity of Handel's music'.

The press in Montagnola is not content simply to rest on this heritage. 'Notwithstanding the use of old types, its books are modern. They are books of our age, and superior in those respects in which our times are pre-eminent. The purely technical aspects, for example, are managed with a refinement unknown to the old master, who printed many a sheet which the modern Officina Bodoni would not release without subjecting it to improvements. Thus the creative spirit of a printer of genius has found, not a mere heir devoid of enterprise, but a worthy and forward looking successor.

'One observation in conclusion: I know that the intellectual content of books is more important than their outward appearance. The niceties of bibliophiles are all very well but do not dispose me to make a special case for them. With the Officina Bodoni it is a matter of specialization, in a narrowly circumscribed field to be sure, but not a trifling one. What compels our admiration and affection is its devotion to an ideal of art and handicraft and an honest and successful striving after perfection'.

7

LUCIUS ANNAEUS SENECA · DE BREVITATE VITAE

Latin text of the 'Dialogus ad Paulinum', chapters I and II.
80 copies on mould-made Fabriano paper.
Set in 20-point Bodoni italic. 12 pages. 21.5 × 15 cm.
Type specimen of the Officina Bodoni: Montagnola, January 1924. (5)
Paper covers, using the same paper as that used for the text. Device on upper cover in red.   Loan

8

JOHANN WOLFGANG GOETHE · DAS ROEMISCHE CARNEVAL 1788

German text from the Weimar 'Sophienausgabe' of Goethe's account of the Roman Carnival, first published in 1789 and later included in his *Italienische Reise* (1830).
6 copies on vellum and 224 on mould-made Fabriano paper.
Set in 20-point Bodoni ornamented italic, a type almost exactly contemporary with the text. 80 pages. 30 × 21 cm.
Editiones Officinae Bodoni: Montagnola, March 1924. (6)   Loan

– Another copy, to show the binding.
Red vellum boards, open device on upper cover, spine faded to natural vellum.
                                                                               Loan

9

WILLIAM SHAKESPEARE · THE TEMPEST

English text of the Cambridge University Press edition.
6 copies on vellum and 224 on mould-made Fabriano paper.
Set in 16-point Bodoni roman and italic. 160 pages. 30×21 cm.
Editiones Officinae Bodoni: Montagnola, July 1924. (7)
White vellum boards, solid device on the upper cover, leather label on spine.

Cup.510.ee.2

– Another copy, to show variant binding: Green vellum boards, open device on
upper cover, black leather label on spine.   Loan

– Prospectus.   Loan

10

ALFRED DE MUSSET · LES NUITS

French text of poems written 1835–37.
5 copies on vellum and 225 on mould-made Marais paper.
Set in 16- and 20-point Bodoni italic. 56 pages. 28.5 × 20 cm.
Editiones Officinae Bodoni: Montagnola, September 1924. (8)
White vellum boards, solid device on upper cover.   Loan

14   ALFRED DE MUSSET

Le Poète

O Muse! spectre insatiable,
Ne m'en demande pas si long.
L'homme n'écrit rien sur le sable
A l'heure où passe l'aquilon.
J'ai vu le temps où ma jeunesse
Sur mes lèvres était sans cesse
Prête à chanter comme un oiseau;
Mais j'ai souffert un dur martyre,
Et le moins que j'en pourrais dire,
Si je l'essayais sur ma lyre,
La briserait comme un roseau.

(MAI 1835)

23

11

UGO FOSCOLO · DEI SEPOLCRI · CARME

Italian text of the poems first published in 1807 and dedicated to Ippolito
Pindemonte, with the poet's notes.
225 copies on mould-made Fabriano paper.
The text set in 20-point Bodoni roman, the notes in 16-point Bodoni roman and
italic. 24 pages. 35×25.5 cm.
Editiones Officinae Bodoni: Montagnola, November 1924. (9)
Grey boards, solid device on upper cover, white cloth spine.   Cup.510.ee.24

– Another copy, to show a variant binding: Red, orange and black marbled paper
boards, white vellum spine.   Loan

Foscolo's Veronese friend Pindemonte had sketched out a poem in which he deplored
the unworthy condition of the cemetery in Verona. Foscolo took over the plan and in
September 1806 composed this deeply-felt hymn to the glorious dead.

12

FRÉDÉRIC LE GRAND
ÉPÎTRE AU MARQUIS D'ARGENS *du 23 septembre 1757*

French text of a letter of Frederick the Great with German translation by Eberhard
König.
224 copies on mould-made Fabriano paper.
Set in 16-point Bodoni roman. 24 pages. 30×21 cm.
Editiones Officinae Bodoni: Montagnola, December 1924. (10)
Blue, grey and red marbled paper boards, white vellum spine.   Loan

13

HANS REINHART · DER SCHATTEN · *Ein Nachtstück aus Andersen*

German text, play in four acts to commemorate the 120th anniversary of the birth
of Hans Christian Andersen.
With an epilogue by the author.
100 copies on mould-made Fabriano paper.
Set in 16-point Bodoni roman and italic. 104 pages. 30×21 cm.
Private edition. Montagnola, February 1925. (11)
Dark grey patterned paper boards, white vellum spine.   Loan

Stanley Morison and Frederic Warde

The first publications of the Officina Bodoni attracted visitors from various countries to Montagnola. Among the first was Stanley Morison, typographic consultant to the Monotype Corporation, who was instrumental in the recutting of a number of the best types of the past and in making them again generally available. Morison wanted specimen pages of the Officina Bodoni's work for inclusion in his *Modern Fine Printing*, and at Christmas 1924 visited Mardersteig to discuss the choice of examples. Mardersteig shared Morison's enthusiasm for the history of the forms of printed letters, and their improvement. The two men became close friends. Morison made Mardersteig aware of the development of early italic types and of the importance of writing-books; Mardersteig acquainted Morison with the methods for constructing Roman capital letters prescribed by the Renaissance antiquary, Felice Feliciano.

A year later Morison introduced Frederic Warde, an American typographer, to Mardersteig. Warde brought to Montagnola in January 1926 the new Arrighi type, modelled on the second printing type of Lodovico degli Arrighi (Vicentino) of Vicenza, scribe and printer. 'Printing the books which I produced with Warde and set in his type provided me with a welcome change, as I had in the meantime begun to tire of the austere and solemn Bodoni types which marked the end of a long development in letter design and did not allow further evolution'.

The Arrighi types

Stanley Morison in his articles in *The Fleuron* maintained that the essential feature of an italic letter is informality rather than slope and that the italic letters of the sixteenth-century writing-master and punch-cutter Lodovico degli Arrighi 'offered a thoroughly practical starting point for designing of an ideal cursive ... harmonious with our classical Old faces'. Morison, already engaged on his programme of type designs for the Monotype Corporation, conceived the plan of realising an 'ideal' italic type, based on Arrighi's first italic type of 1524, to be first engraved by hand on steel punches in the traditional way. Together he and Warde commissioned a punch-cutter, Charles Plumet, in Paris to cut the new face; and to strike and justify the matrices.

The new type was cast in Paris by the typefounders Ribadeau Dumas and was first used by Warde and Morison to print Robert Bridges's *The Tapestry* at the Fanfare Press in London in 1924. It was first used at the Officina Bodoni to print Morison's introduction to *The Calligraphic Models of Ludovico degli Arrighi*. Alternative forms of b d h k and l were cut in Paris by Charles Malin in 1926 in which the ascenders end in serifs instead of blobs. The first full showing of this variant, known as 'Vicenza', was in the Officina Bodoni edition of Plato's *Crito*.

14

a

LUDOVICO VICENTINO
The Calligraphic Models of Ludovico degli Arrighi surnamed Vicentino
A Complete Facsimile edited by Stanley Morison

Facsimile edition of the Italian original, comprising the two parts: 'La Operina di Ludouico Vicentino, da imparare di scriuere littera Cancellarescha', Rome, 1522, and 'Il modo di temperare le Penne con le uarie Sorti di littere ordinato per Ludouico Vicentino', Rome, 1523. Introduction in English by Stanley Morison.
300 copies on mould-made J. W. Zanders paper.
The introduction set in Arrighi 'Vicentino' 16-point italic. Introduction 16 pages; facsimile 64 pages. 25×15.5 cm.
Printed for Frederic Warde, Paris. Montagnola, March 1926. (15)
Fawn linen.   Cup.510.ee.3

This is the first of several facsimile editions of Renaissance writing-books printed by the Officina Bodoni.

b

– Proof copy (incomplete) of *The Calligraphic Models*.   Loan

Throughout this paste-up are notes and remarks in the hand of Frederic Warde, probably addressed to Stanley Morison. The colophon is in Warde's pencilled hand ('T . . . hundred copies printed privately for Frederic Warde at the Officina Bodoni, Montagnola, March 1926'). But at Mardersteig's request it was altered to read, 'For and under the direction of Frederic Warde . . .'; Mardersteig was responsible for the printing only.

c

Prospectus for *The Calligraphic Models of Ludovico degli Arrighi*.

Printed on mould-made Fabriano wove paper. 25.5×18 cm.   Loan

Early in 1926 this prospectus for *The Calligraphic Models* was set up in the Arrighi type of Frederic Warde. The book itself, however, printed in March of that year, had a different imprint and a different format, and a more thorough introduction.

The prospectus has the imprint 'Florence Academia Typographica 1926'; John Dreyfus records that the idea of moving to Italy had then already been in Mardersteig's mind for several months. He had even gone as far as proofing a prospectus for a new 'Accademia Tipographica' which he and Warde were planning to set up in Florence. When he won the competition for the D'Annunzio national edition Mardersteig decided instead to settle in Verona, and the move to Verona did not, in fact, take place until Spring 1927.

The Preface to the published book was printed unaltered from the setting of the prospectus, without deleting the words 'of which the present pages are a prospectus'; and so in the bound volumes the Preface leaf had to be cancelled.

PREFACE

The volume, of which the present pages are a prospectus embraces the complete series of calligraphic models made and published by Ludovico degli Arrighi. The facsimiles have been taken from the first edition of his two works and are in the size of the originals. Considerable care has been taken with the reproductions to preserve as far as possible the splendour of the original plates. It is hoped that they may be of some service to students of typography and calligraphy; it may be, too, that artists and designers will find in the same models an inspiration towards beautiful writing and lettering.

The type used in this volume is based upon the cursive designed by Arrighi and first used in his "Coryciana," Rome, mdxxiv.

The punches for the type have been cut by hand.

The printing has been done on the hand-presses of the Officina Bodoni at Montagnola, upon specially watermarked paper. Also the binding is made entirely by hand with vellum back and with figured paper covered boards made expressly for this book.

Only Three Hundred copies printed.

15

CRITO · A SOCRATIC DIALOGUE BY PLATO

English translation by Henry Cary.
5 copies on Japanese vellum and 475 on mould-made Binda paper.
Set in Arrighi 'Vicenza' 16-point italic. 38 pages. 23 × 15 cm.
Printed for 'The Pleiad, Paris'. Montagnola, May 1926. (16)
Muted red-brown and grey marbled paper boards.

Copy No. 475.   Cup.510.ee.4

Printed under the supervision of Frederic Warde. Although the colophon states that this was the first use of 'Vicenza', his Arrighi type with modified ascenders, which terminate in serifs instead of blobs, 'Vicenza' was in fact used in the imprint and colophon of *The Calligraphic Models*, March 1926.

– Another copy, to show the variant binding.   Loan
Muted red-brown and brown-green marbled paper boards.

Thus the whole circle of travellers may
be reduced to the following heads: —

IDLE TRAVELLERS,
INQUISITIVE TRAVELLERS,
LYING TRAVELLERS,
PROUD TRAVELLERS,
VAIN TRAVELLERS,
SPLENETIC TRAVELLERS;

then follow

THE TRAVELLERS OF NECESSITY,
THE DELINQUENT AND FELONIOUS
TRAVELLER,
THE UNFORTUNATE AND INNOCENT
TRAVELLER,
THE SIMPLE TRAVELLER,

And last of all (if you please)

THE SENTIMENTAL TRAVELLER

(meaning thereby myself), who have
travelled, and of which I am now sitting
down to give an account, — as much out

[9]

Sterne, *An excerpt from 'A Sentimental Journey'* (1926). Specimen of Bodoni's Cuneo. (16)

16

LAWRENCE [sic] STERNE · *An excerpt from*
A SENTIMENTAL JOURNEY

A first specimen of 12-point Cuneo Bodoni roman and italic. English text of the
chapter 'In the Desobligeant'.
25 copies. 16 pages, plus 8 pages blank at each end. 20 × 13 cm.
Officina Bodoni: Montagnola, May 1926.
Red, orange and black marbled paper boards, paper label on spine.   Loan

In an extended colophon Mardersteig expressed his disappointment over the post-
ponement of his projected visit to England because of the General Strike: 'A journey,
it would seem, is at the mercy of political factions, not sentiment, which is the motive
of all good journeys. In a sentiment of admiring affection for the heroic island where
I hope to journey – when railway wheels should move again – this greeting was
printed with Giambattista Bodoni's twelve-point type Cuneo, here used for the first
time since his death'.

17

HORACE WALPOLE · HIEROGLYPHIC TALES

English text; six tales with an epilogue and notes by the author, after the first
edition of six copies printed at Strawberry Hill, Twickenham in 1785.
250 copies on Binda mould-made paper.
Set in 12-point Bodoni roman and italic. 88 pages. 23.5 × 16 cm.
Printed for Elkin Mathews, London. Montagnola, September 1926. (17)
Dark brown trellis-patterned paper boards, paper label on spine.   Cup.510.ee.5

18

CARLO RICKETTS · DELL'ARTE DELLA STAMPA

Italian translation of 'A Defence of the Revival of Printing', by Charles Ricketts (1899).
125 copies on mould-made Marais paper.
Set in 12-point Bodoni roman and italic. 44 pages. 20 × 13.5 cm.
Private edition for Stabilimenti Grafici Mondadori a Verona. Montagnola,
December 1926 (18)
Muted green, brown and yellow marbled paper boards, white vellum spine.

Cup.510.ee.6

The preface to the Officina Bodoni edition states: 'The author of this little book, Charles Ricketts, fruitfully collaborated on his Vale Press in the revival of fine printing in England at almost the same time as William Morris. These explanatory pages of a guiding aesthetic which is inspired by the great models of the printers of our Renaissance, as opposed to that of the gothic and mediaevalist William Morris, are a contribution to the critical discussion of the art of fine printing'.

19

THE POETICAL WORKS OF PHILIP DORMER STANHOPE EARL OF CHESTERFIELD

English text; poems and epigrams with notes by the editor, from volume III of the edition of the 'Miscellaneous Works', London, 1778, with the addition of a few poems from other sources.
250 copies on mould-made Binda paper.
Set in 12-point Bodoni roman. 48 pages. 23.5 × 16 cm.
Printed for Elkin Mathews & Marrot Ltd., London. Montagnola, January 1927. (19)
Indigo trellis-patterned paste-paper boards, paper label on spine

Copy No. 233. Cup.510.ee.7

20

DAMIANUS MOYLLUS
A newly discovered Treatise on Classic Letter Design. Printed at Parma by Damianus Moyllus circa 1480. Reproduced in facsimile with an Introduction by Stanley Morison.

Facsimile edition of the only known copy of the first printed treatise on the geometrical construction of Roman capital letters.
350 copies on mould-made Arches paper. The introduction and translation set in 13-point Poliphilus & Blado. 84 pages; 18.5 × 12.5 cm. (pp. 27–74: facsimile in collotype by Albert Frisch, Berlin).
Printed for the Pegasus Press: Paris. Montagnola, January 1927. (20)
Blue Ingres paper boards, Moyllus letters A and Z gold-blocked on upper and lower covers (the Z is inverted), vellum spine. Cup.510.ee.8

– Another copy, to show the binding. Loan

Damianus Moyllus, a stationer, miniaturist and calligrapher of Parma published *c.* 1480 the first printed treatise on the geometrical construction of capital letters, using the circle and the square. This little book was printed on one side of the sheet only and unbound, possibly because it was intended for use by craftsmen.

Morison notes that the idea of a perfect letter, possessing a fixed proportion, was later rigorously systematized in France by Geofroy Tory and others. The mathematical construction of letter forms was in 1692 raised to an unprecedented level of precision, when the Académie des Sciences designed for the Imprimerie Royale a set of drawings laid out on a grid of 2,304 squares. The engraver refused to adhere to them, insisting that the eye was the sovereign creator and arbiter of form; a principle, incidentally, which Mardersteig observed in his own type designs.

21

BEETHOVENS HEILIGENSTÄDTER TESTAMENT

German text of Beethoven's will, written at Heiligenstadt on 2 October 1802, with the codicil of 10 October.
33 copies on mould-made Marais paper.
Set in 20-point Bodoni. 16 pages. 28.5 × 19.5 cm.
Private edition 'Amicis'. Montagnola, March 1927. (21)
Green and brown marbled paper boards, vellum spine. Headbands in green.
This copy was printed for Stanley Morison.   Loan

Francesco Pastonchi and Arnoldo Mondadori

Among Mardersteig's visitors was the poet, literary historian and bibliophile, Francesco Pastonchi. 'Stimulated, like myself, by the writing-books of the sixteenth century he had a type-face designed for a new series of Italian classics. He hoped to enlist me for the printing of this collection which never developed beyond the stage of a project, but at least I could help him have the Pastonchi type-face cut by Monotype. Pastonchi seldom came to Montagnola alone; he used to bring bibliophiles and publishers, including Arnoldo Mondadori, to whom he showed the hand press with the pride of a discoverer'. It was through Mondadori that Mardersteig was invited to take part in a competition organised by the Italian government for printing a national edition of the works of Gabriele D'Annunzio, then regarded as Italy's foremost poet.

Gabriele D'Annunzio

'Gabriele D'Annunzio was an extraordinary personality, a figure of the Renaissance, at once poet and condottiere, who had created for himself his own fantastic world'. In the garden of the Vittoriale, his villa overlooking Lake Garda, he had installed his aeroplane and even a destroyer, high and dry. From this ship D'Annunzio fired a salute of thirteen guns to mark Mardersteig's first visit and the beginning of the printing of his complete works.

Despite the great differences in their ages and tastes, Mardersteig got on well with D'Annunzio who responded to all his typographical suggestions. 'I once showed him the first page of one of his texts on which an abundance of commas created a confusing effect and I asked him to eliminate some. He looked at the sheet, paused for a moment and agreed – *"Via con questi vermicelli!"* ("Away with these worms!"). It was difficult to prevent him from removing every comma'.

D'Annunzio, the poet of the florid, the flamboyant and the theatrical, saw his own writings appear in a guise of classic plainness and perfection, relying for its effect solely on the beauty of its letter forms and the sobriety of their presentation. D'Annunzio called Mardersteig 'Prince of Printers'.

The D'Annunzio national edition

Mardersteig's prospectus and specimens printed in Bodoni types won the competition, and in 1927 he moved to Italy. 'At the suggestion of Arnoldo Mondadori a courtyard in his great printing house in Verona was roofed over and there the Officina Bodoni . . . installed a separate department for the production of the D'Annunzio edition. The hand press was used only for a special edition on Japanese vellum and for the printing of copies on vellum . . . whereas the normal edition was to be printed on machines installed for this purpose'.

This formidable task occupied the Officina Bodoni almost completely until the completion of the D'Annunzio national edition in 1936; between 1933 and 1935 no other books were printed on the hand press. Mardersteig was nevertheless experimenting with Monotype faces such as Garamond, Bembo and Poliphilus and acquired additional hand presses for printing copper engravings and lithographs.

In 1937 the Officina Bodoni was removed from the Mondadori plant to Mardersteig's spacious house in the Via Marsala, overlooking the city of Verona.

22

a

GABRIELE D'ANNUNZIO
LAUDI DEL CIELO · DEL MARE · DELLA TERRA · E DEGLI EROI
Libro terzo · ALCIONE

2501 copies printed on Fabriano paper in the Verona printing house of Arnoldo
Mondadori. 209 copies on Japanese vellum and nine copies on vellum printed on
the hand press. 24.5 × 16.5 cm. Set in Bodoni types.
Istituto Nazionale per la Edizione di tutte le Opere di Gabriele D'Annunzio.
Officina Bodoni: Verona, May 1927.   Copy No. 103.   012227.de.1

For five years Mardersteig was occupied with the production of the forty-nine volumes,
many of them of 500 pages or more, all set by hand in Bodoni types. 218 copies were
printed on the hand press; and also an edition of 2501 copies was printed by machine
under Mardersteig's supervision, of which a volume is exhibited here.

Printing on the machine with Bodoni's original types was difficult because the
sharply cut serifs of the letters were not suitable for printing at speed on a machine
press. After a few hundred copies the press was stopped in order to change letters
that had become damaged. To replace some particularly weak letters by accurate
but more resistant recuttings Mardersteig commissioned the punch-cutter Charles
Malin. 'He accomplished his task with great skill, for his recuttings cannot be distinguished from the originals even under strong magnification'.

b

Tutte le Opere di Gabriele D'Annunzio. (Programma)

Edited by Angelo Sodini. Printed by Hans Mardersteig and Remo Mondadori under
the direction of Arnoldo Mondadori.
100 copies *ad personam* and 500 numbered copies. 32 × 21.5 cm.
Set in Bodoni types.
Istituto Nazionale per la Edizione di tutte le Opere di Gabriele D'Annunzio:
Milan. Officina Bodoni: Verona, June 1927.   Loan

This prospectus or 'programme volume', formed part of the national edition of
D'Annunzio's works. It contains specimen pages, facsimiles, photographs, and other
illustrations.

23

THE PASTONCHI FACE
A Specimen of a new Letter for Use on the 'Monotype'

English text, with an introduction by Hans Mardersteig, three illustrations,
13 specimen pages of prose and verse in various sizes and layouts of a new type-face
designed by Eduardo Cotti under the direction of the Italian poet Francesco
Pastonchi, and cut by the Monotype Corporation.
200 copies on mould-made Fabriano paper.
Set on the Monotype in the Pastonchi face. 70 pages. 29 × 20.5 cm.
Composed and printed for The Lanston Monotype Corporation, London,
according to the design of Hans Mardersteig at the Veronese Press of Arnoldo
Mondadori by the Officina Bodoni, Verona, Spring 1928. (24)
Brown cloth, title in Pastonchi letters on upper cover.   Cup.510.ee.10

24

ANDRES BRUN · CALLIGRAPHER OF SARAGOSSA
*Some Account of his Life and Work by Henry Thomas & Stanley Morison. With a
facsimile in collotype of the surviving text and plates of his two writing books
1583 & 1612.*

Facsimile edition of the writing books by the Spanish calligrapher Andres Brun,
from the copies preserved in the Kunstgewerbe-Museum, Berlin. With an
introduction by Henry Thomas and a note by Stanley Morison. The facsimile in
collotype in black and red by Albert Frisch, Berlin.
175 copies on Fabriano mould-made paper.
Set in 14- and 12-point Janson roman and italic. 32 pages of text.
The 48 pages of the facsimile were numbered by hand in pencil by Stanley
Morison. 31 × 22 cm.
Printed for The Pegasus Press, Paris. Verona, November 1928. (Dated in the
colophon November 1928 but on the title-page 1929.) (26)
Fine-weave oatmeal cloth, blocked in red with Brun arabesque border on upper
and lower cover and spine.   Copy No. 83.   Cup.510.ee.11

– Another copy.   Copy No. 175.   Loan

The introduction to this facsimile edition, published by John Holroyd Reece's Pegasus
Press, was written by Morison's friend Dr Henry (later Sir Henry) Thomas of the
Department of Printed Books, British Museum.

Andres Brun (1929). Title-page, and facsimile of a page of his woodcut writing book. (24)

25

EVSTACHIO CELEBRINO DA VDENE

Calligrapher, Engraver and Writer for the Venetian Printing Press, by Stanley Morison.
With Illustrations in the text and a complete collotype facsimile of 'The way of learning
to write the Lettera Merchantescha by Eustachio Celebrino, 1525'.

Facsimile edition of the writing book designed and engraved by Eustachio
Cellebrino of Udine: 'Il modo di imparare di scriuere lettera merchantescha', etc.
With a note in English on the life and work of the calligrapher and engraver by
Stanley Morison and 7 illustrations.
175 copies on hand-made Montval paper.
The text set in 13-point Poliphilus & Blado: 30 pages, 25 × 17 cm. The facsimile
in collotype: 8 pages, 15.5 × 10.5 cm.
Printed for The Pegasus Press, Paris. Verona, January 1929. (29)
Black fine-weave cloth, title in gold on upper cover, with flourishes above and
below, top edge gilt, green headbands.   Copy No. 128.   Cup.510.ee.12

26

THE OFFICINA BODONI
The Operation of a Handpress during the first six years of its work.

Catalogue raisonné of all books printed on the hand press of the Officina Bodoni from 1923 to 1929, with an introduction, 'The Apologia of the Officina Bodoni' by Hans Mardersteig. The essay 'How a book is made at the Officina Bodoni' is illustrated with twelve woodcuts by Frans Masereel (1889–1972) showing the processes by which a book is set by hand, printed on the hand press, and bound. Eight specimen pages of books published and five reproductions, in heliogravure and collotype, of documents, portraits, facsimiles and (in black, red and blue) the various forms of the printer's device.
English edition: 500 copies on Lafuma paper with the specimen pages and documents on various hand-made papers.
The text is set in 14- and 12-point Bodoni; the specimen pages in 12-, 16- and 20-point Bodoni, 16-point Arrighi 'Vicentino' & 'Vicenza', and 12-point Pastonchi. 82 pages. 30×21 cm.
Editiones Officinae Bodoni; At the sign of the Pegasus: Paris, New York. Verona, Summer 1929. (30)
Natural linen, solid device on upper cover, top edge gilt, scarlet headbands.

Copy No. 109.   Cup.510.ee.13

– Another copy.

Copy No. 24.   Loan

German and Italian editions were also published.

The check-list of books printed by the Press lists thirty-three items, together with fourteen titles from the complete works of D'Annunzio. Of the twenty-one books printed at Montagnola between 1923 and 1927 on the hand press of the Officina Bodoni, six were printed for other publishers, four were private editions, one was a type specimen of the press, and ten were issued under its own imprint (although the wording 'Editiones Officinae Bodoni' was not used until 1929, on the title-page of this book).

'How a book is made at the Officina Bodoni'

In *The Officina Bodoni* (1929) Mardersteig described clearly and succinctly the processes by which a book is made at the Officina Bodoni. His account, illustrated with twelve woodcuts by Frans Masereel, was reissued in 1973. This is the text:

THE TEXT: COPY EDITING

'All texts before being set up are thoroughly examined. The best critical edition is chosen, and if it does not agree with the latest research, a new revised text is established by comparison with the original manuscript or the first edition. When the copy has thus been prepared it is worked through from the typographic point of view from title-page to colophon and got ready, that is: provided with all the necessary directions for the compositor'.

TYPE SETTING

'The compositor picks out each letter from the typecase, which is divided into about a hundred small compartments for upper-case, lower-case, signs of punctuation and spaces, and inserts it in the composing-stick. Before him is the copy, and near him a tray into which he transfers the completed lines from the composing-stick until a page is finished. This page is sometimes bound round with string. Good setting demands careful work, for in hand-press printing it is not so much speed of execution, as evenness of spacing and the avoidance of too frequent divisions of words, which determine the beauty of the page'.

'Every four to eight pages are placed together in the forme on the bed of the press. The text is read for corrections at least five times. The removal of letters which are defective from casting or from use takes place on the machine before the beginning of the printing and the last reading. Finally the forme is secured with wedges (quoins) and furniture until it forms one solid block as though all the letters had been cast together'.

PAPER

'Hand-made laid papers, in which the wire-lines of the sieve can be seen, or wove papers, which look like vellum when held against the light, are damped in order to make them more pliant. The lightly damped sheet is pinned by the pressman to a frame covered with paper or other material, and in printing this frame is folded down on to the forme'.

'MAKE-READY'

'Then comes the most troublesome task, the make-ready, which means the removal of unevenness in the impression. The first pull of a sheet, in which the impression is unequal, partly too black and partly too grey, owing to inevitable minute unevennesses in the bed of the press, the platen or the types, is corrected by the use of tissue paper until a perfectly uniform impression is obtained. Finally the register-sheet is placed in the frame between the platen and the corrected forme in such a manner that the sheet is accurately superimposed upon the printing surface. A perfect and harmonious impression can be obtained only by such means. In the hand press several register-sheets are laid one upon the other until the slightest deviation in colour is eliminated'.

INKING

'Each sheet must be inked by hand with the roller; the art of the hand-printer consists in securing evenness of colour and the correct mean between too much and too little ink. After inking, the frame is folded down upon the forme and the bed is brought under the platen of the press'.

PRINTING

'Now comes the printing. By pulling the bar or lever the platen is brought down on to the forme. A sharp eye is needed to examine each separate pull, and the work further involves considerable muscular effort, especially if prose composition completely occupies the printing forme.

The daily production of a hand press when used with care amounts to about 200–300 sheets printed on one side. If the other side has been printed on the previous day, the sheets can be hung up to dry'.

SEWING

'After drying, the sheets are pressed to remove the relief caused on the reverse side of the sheet by the impression of the type. They are then sorted, checked, folded and gathered into the sewing-rack, where they are sewn'.

BINDING

'Precious books are bound in calf vellum or in morocco, the hide of goats from Morocco or the Cape. Hand-made bindings are decorated by the gilder on both covers, the spine, outside and inside edges by means of punches or rollers.

And finally the volumes are submitted to the examining touch and the critical eye of the collectors'.

The Officina Bodoni device

Mardersteig described the Christian origin of the device as the orb surmounted by the cross. The bull's horns are the printer's personal addition. The device has been used at different times in various forms and different colours.

Examples of various devices used by the Officina Bodoni.

27

GERARDUS MERCATOR

The Treatise of Gerard Mercator. Literarum Latinarum, quas Italicas, cursoriasque vocant, scribendarum ratio. (Antwerp 1540). Edited in Facsimile with an Introduction by Jan Denucé, Antwerp, and a Note by Stanley Morison, London.

A facsimile edition of the writing book by the great cartographic publisher, Mercator, prepared as a model for his workshop staff.
200 copies on Fabriano mould-made paper.
Text set in 10-point Janson. Introduction 14 pages, facsimile 56 pages. 20×14 cm.
Printed for 'De Sikkel', Antwerp and the Pegasus Press, Paris. Verona, March 1930. (33)
Green fine-weave cloth, title on upper cover surrounded by flourishes, top edge gilt, yellow and black headbands.   Copy No. 53.   Cup.510.ee.14

– Another copy.   Copy No. 30.   Loan

28

P. OVIDII NASONIS AMORES
Qui fuerant quinque libelli sunt tres.

Latin text of the Teubner edition, Leipzig, 1886, edited by R. Ehwald. Initials drawn by hand, in red, by Claudio Bonacini.
3 copies on vellum and 120 on mould-made Magnani paper.
Set in 16-point Vicenza italic. 142 pages. 24×16 cm.
Editiones Officinae Bodoni: Verona, February 1932. (35)
Natural linen, title on upper cover surrounded by flourishes, top edge gilt, red headbands.   Copy No. 7.   Loan

The printing on Magnani paper marks the beginning of a long collaboration with the Cartiera Magnani in Pescia.

   Mardersteig recalled that a prospectus was printed for the *Crito* (1926) on a dry, hard-surfaced paper as opposed to damp paper, and that the breakage of kerns, particularly on the lower-case y, was so great that his Vicenza fount was depleted. The Ovid text, in Latin, fortunately needed few y's.

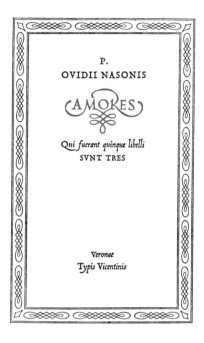

Ovid, *Amores* (1932). Title-page. Set in Vicenza italic. (28)

29

MAURICE SANDOZ · PERSONAL REMARKS ABOUT ENGLAND
Essays by a Swiss boy in his best English.

250 copies printed in red and black on Fabriano paper.
Set in 12-point Baskerville. 161 pages. 19 × 12 cm.
Private edition for the Libreria Dante: Verona, December 1932.
White imitation vellum boards.

Copy No. 19.   Loan

30

GABRIELE D'ANNUNZIO · L'OLEANDRO
Con litografie di G. G. Boehmer, Mcmxxxvi.

Italian text of a poem from 'Alcione' illustrated with 26 lithographs, printed in sanguine, by Gunter Böhmer.
180 copies: 20 on Kaji Torinoko nacred Japanese paper, of which the first five contain a second suite of the lithographs printed in blue; 160 on mould-made Marais paper, and 10 on various hand-made papers.
Set in 20-point Bodoni italic. 34 pages. 36×26.5 cm.
Editiones Officinae Bodoni: Verona, July 1936. (37)
Inserted loose in a publisher's buckram cover.

Copy No. 70. Lent by the Bodleian Library, Oxford.

On the completion of the D'Annunzio edition Mardersteig installed the hand press in his villa and widened the scope and technique of his work by acquiring a lithographic press and copper-plate press. 'As my first illustrated book I would like to mention D'Annunzio's *Oleandro*, illustrated by Gunter Böhmer with lithographs drawn on the stone in red crayon. Here I used for the first time an italic Bodoni fount (*Casale*) which harmonised well with the lithographs'.

Fontana

In 1935–36 Mardersteig worked for a year in Glasgow for the Collins Cleartype Press. John Dreyfus relates (*On the work of Giovanni Mardersteig with 'Monotype' faces*): 'One of his first questions on arrival was "May I see your clear type?" It was explained to him that no such type existed, although all their types were in fact clear. This did not satisfy Mardersteig who suggested that if they called themselves a Cleartype Press they ought to have a type which would distinguish them from other printers. A type of Scottish origin seemed to be indicated and his choice fell upon a type used in Glasgow by Foulis in the eighteenth century'.

Thus the new type, later called Fontana, was derived from that of Alexander Wilson (1714–86) of the Glasgow Letter Foundry, with letters slightly wider and more open than Baskerville's. 'The Monotype Corporation agreed to make the type under Mardersteig's direction for the exclusive use of Collins. Nevertheless he was allowed to use it himself for an edition of Walter Savage Landor's *Imaginary Conversations* which he designed and printed for The Limited Editions Club of New York, whose founder (George Macy) considered it to be one of the ten finest books he had ever published'. Collins in 1961 gave permission for the unrestricted sale of this type to other printers.

31

WALTER SAVAGE LANDOR · IMAGINARY CONVERSATIONS
Selected, with an introduction by R. H. Boothroyd.

1,500 copies.
Set in Monotype Fontana and printed at the Officina Bodoni, Verona.
Limited Editions Club: New York, 1936.   C.105.d.12

Fontana was designed by Mardersteig for the exclusive use of Collins Cleartype Press, and for this book alone he was allowed to use it himself.

32

DUE EPISODI DELLA VITA DI FELICE FELICIANO
Ovvero la terza e decimaquarta novella da 'Le Porretane' di Sabbadino degli Arienti.

Italian text; two anecdotes of the life of Felice Feliciano of Verona, from the 'Novelle Porretane', written in 1478 by Sabbadino degli Arienti, with a Note by Hans Mardersteig.
First specimen of a new type-face called Griffo, engraved by Charles Malin after the type cut by Francesco Griffo for the Aldine edition of Pietro Bembo's *De Aetna* (1495).
35 copies on mould-made Binda paper.
Set in 16-point Griffo roman and italic. 16 pages. 23.5×16.5 cm.
Editiones Officinae Bodoni: Verona, September 1939. (41)
Vellum-coloured Linson with open device on upper cover, grey cloth label on spine.   Loan

Griffo

Mardersteig's first type design was cut in 1929 but did not appear publicly for another ten years. It was, like Morison's 'Monotype' Bembo, modelled on the roman type cut by Francesco Griffo for Aldus Manutius, which was first used in Pietro Bembo's *De Aetna* (1495).

Mardersteig explained: 'Despite the excellence of Monotype Bembo, Morison regretted that in the mechanical recutting something of the supple elegance of the original had been lost. When I talked to Morison about my plan to have a fine old type recut by that wonderful punch-cutter Charles Malin for use on my hand press, Morison strongly advised me to take the *De Aetna* type as a model too'. Mardersteig followed this advice with some reluctance: 'I had little inclination to compete with the extremely serviceable recutting by Monotype. A comparison with the original letters, however, convinced me that Morison was right'.

Malin spent a few months in Mardersteig's home in Verona and there he recut the *De Aetna* roman, working from a copy of the Aldine edition (1495) lent by Tammaro De Marinis. To distinguish it from Monotype Bembo, Mardersteig called this recutting 'Griffo', after its original creator. 'Every evening we examined and discussed the "smokes" – that is, the impressions obtained by blackening the face of the newly-cut punches with soot from a candle. These we compared with the print of the original'. Mardersteig shared Morison's belief that the 1495 *De Aetna* was to be considered as a kind of type specimen, because on each page of this short book are several examples of variant forms of the same letter, e.g. up to five for the letter e. He relates: 'Only later when I could examine a large number of Griffo's types and understood his individual style did I arrive at an entirely different explanation'.

Griffo was guided by the same thought as Gutenberg – to get as close in his type designs to contemporary handwriting as possible; in this case, to the humanistic letters which were the starting point for all the types we call roman. Griffo, therefore, cut several slightly different 'sorts' of a, e and m. In imitation of manuscript practice he even supplied some of his letters with deliberate copies of calligraphic flourishes; and with the same intention he provided the first italic type with a profusion of ligatures.

In recutting the Griffo type for modern printing a choice had to be made among these variant letter forms. It was not easy to select the best versions for Malin to follow because they were nearly all good. Defects of casting in some letters in the 1495 volume and the over-inking of many pages complicated this choice.

A trial fount was cast, and when Morison compared the first trial setting with Monotype Bembo he found that the fount cut by hand was far closer to the original than the version cut for mechanical composition. Nevertheless Mardersteig points out that Monotype Bembo 'has the advantage of being more suitable for general use because of its variations from the original model, some of them made for technical reasons and others in order to produce a more regular appearance'. He continues: 'The Griffo type used at the Officina Bodoni . . . was the subject of a number of minor improvements in the years which followed its first introduction'. The second state of Griffo was first shown in 1960. 'It may be said that it comes closer to the original and retains more of its elegance without being an exact copy – a thing which it never claimed to be'. The Griffo italic was based on a cursive type cut late in his career by Griffo *c.* 1507, probably at Fano for the printer Soncino.

33

TORQUATO TASSO · AMINTA · *Favola boscareccia.*

Italian text of Tasso's fable, written in 1573. Illustrated with seven etchings by
Francesco Chiappelli.
120 copies on mould-made Magnani paper.
Set in 16-point Griffo. 130 pages. 29×20 cm.
Printed for the Cento Amici del Libro, Florence. Verona, December 1939. (42)
Yellow Ingres paper boards with cream paper labels printed in mauve, pasted on
upper cover and spine. Top edge coloured yellow, mauve headbands.

Copy No. XVIII.   Loan

Although the colophon states that this was the first book to be printed in Griffo, *Due
episodi della vita di Felice Feliciano* (September 1939) was the first specimen of the new
design. *Aminta* was certainly the first book printed by the Officina Bodoni for I Cento
Amici del Libro, founded by Tammaro De Marinis, Ugo Ojetti and the Marchesa
Gilberta Serlupi Crescenzi. This society was of special importance to the Officina
Bodoni when the usual export outlets were no longer available after the outbreak
of the Second World War. Each of the hundred members of the society had his
name printed in swash letters below the colophon in his copy. Twenty extra copies
were numbered I–XX. Mardersteig remained responsible for the design and printing
of all the society's publications until his retirement in 1974.

34

GIOVANNI BOCCACCIO · IL NINFALE FIESOLANO
*Con le figure di una perduta edizione fiorentina del quattrocento ora riunite da vari libri
del cinquecento e reincise in legno.*

Italian text, poem in stanzas written about 1344–1346, with a foreword by
Tammaro De Marinis. Illustrated with 22 woodcuts engraved by Fritz Kredel after
those of Bartolomeo di Giovanni. A reconstruction of a lost illustrated edition
printed in Florence towards the end of the fifteenth century. All the woodcuts have
here been reassembled: sixteen of them were used for an edition of the 'Ninfale
fiesolano' published in 1568 at Florence by Valente Panizza; six others were found
in various works published during the sixteenth century.
110 copies on mould-made Magnani paper. The text set in 12-point Bembo italic,
the foreword in roman. 84 pages. 27.5×20 cm.
Editiones Officinae Bodoni: Verona, February 1940. (43)
White vellum, white headbands. By Giannini, Florence.

Cup.510.ee.15

35

BEETHOVENS HEILIGENSTÄDTER TESTAMENT

German text of Beethoven's will, written at Heiligenstadt on 2 October 1802, with
the codicil of 10 October 1802.
300 copies on mould-made Magnani paper.
Set in 16-point Zeno. 16 pages. 26×17 cm.
Printed for the Johannes Asmus Verlag, Leipzig. Verona, August 1940. (44)
Dark blue Ingres paper boards, vellum spine, top edge gilt, blue headbands.   Loan

36

RAINER MARIA RILKE · LETTRES À UNE AMIE VÉNITIENNE

First edition of 34 letters to Mimi Romanelli (32 in French and two in German);
with a vignette on the title-page etched by Mario Vellani-Marchi.
420 copies on mould-made Magnani paper.
Set in 16-point Griffo italic. 86 pages. 25×17 cm.
Printed for Erardo Aeschlimann, Milan, and the Johannes Asmus Verlag,
Leipzig. Verona, October 1941. (49)
White vellum, semi-limp boards with yapped fore-edges, top edge gilt, red
headbands.   Copy No. XLI.   Loan

*Ces lettres jusqu'à présent inédites, composées en
italiques Griffo, ont été imprimées à la presse à
bras en quatre cent vingt exemplaires sur papier
vélin à la cuve de Magnani, dont cinquante exemplaires hors commerce marqués I-L pour le pro-
priétaire des lettres, M. E. Aeschlimann à Milan.
Des exemplaires numérotés 1-350, cent cinquante
ont été réservés à l'éditeur Ulrico Hoepli à Milan,
et deux cents à l'éditeur Johannes Asmus à Leipzig. Vingt exemplaires de service ne sont pas numérotés. Aucun changement n'a été apporté au texte
original, mais quelques fautes d'orthographe ont
été corrigées. La vignette du titre a été gravée à
l'eau-forte par Mario Vellani-Marchi.*
Officina Bodoni, Verona
Octobre 1941 · xx

Exemplaire Nº XLI

37

IL CASTELLO DI MONSELICE
RACCOLTA DEGLI ANTICHI LIBRI VENEZIANI FIGURATI
descritta da Tammaro De Marinis.

Italian text. Catalogue of the collection of Venetian illustrated books of the
fifteenth and sixteenth centuries at the castle of Monselice; with 10 reproductions
in the text, 92 plates in heliogravure, one facsimile and a bibliography.
310 copies on hand-made Magnani paper.
Set in 13-point Bembo; some of the titles in Gothic types. xiv+406 pages.
32×24.5 cm.
Private edition. Verona, December 1941. (50)
Half-vellum, marbled paper boards, red leather label on spine, top edge gilt.   Loan

38

MASSIMO BONTEMPELLI · VIAGGIO D'EUROPA

Italian text; novel. Illustrated with 23 lithographs by Arturo Martini.
175 copies; 5 printed on Japanese vellum and signed by the artist and 170 on
mould-made Fabriano paper.
Set in 20-point Garamond. 102 pages. 40×29 cm.
Printed for the Edizioni della Chimera, Milan. Verona, April 1942. (52)
Copy printed on Japanese vellum.
Unbound set of folded quires.
                    Copy No. II printed for Rudolf Freiherr von Simolin.   Loan

39

CECCO ANGIOLIERI · SONETTE

Italian text of the 150 sonnets by Cecco Angiolieri of Siena (*c.* 1260–*c.* 1312) with
German prose translation by Rudolf Freiherr von Simolin, Hans Rheinfelder and
Otto Freiherr von Taube; followed by a biographical sketch and a commentary.
165 copies on mould-made Magnani paper.
Set in 16-point Griffo, the sonnets in roman, the translation in italic. 358 pages.
28.5×20 cm.
Private edition for Rudolf Freiherr von Simolin. Verona (1943–1944), May 1944. (60)
Green and black patterned paper boards, cloth spine with paper label. Yellow
top edge, fawn headbands.
                    Copy No. 48.   Cup.510.ee.33

40

RUDOLF HAGELSTANGE · VENEZIANISCHES CREDO

German text; first edition of the 35 sonnets, of which 24 were written at Venice,
4 at Breganze and 7 at Verona.
155 copies on mould-made Fabriano paper.
Set in 16-point Griffo roman and italic. 44 pages. 28 × 19 cm.
Editiones Officinae Bodoni: Verona, April 1945. (67)
Dark blue paper boards with vellum spine, top edge gilt, blue headbands.   Loan

These sonnets were circulated clandestinely under the Nazi régime during the last
months of the war. In March 1945 Mardersteig was deeply impressed by them when
they were shown to him in an anonymous manuscript. His offer to print them, provided he could reveal the author's name, was accepted.

   Mardersteig in a letter to John Ryder reported that a good many copies of this
edition had to be destroyed because of defects in the paper, made at the end of the
war, which only became visible after printing.

41

PAUL VALÉRY · LE CIMETIÈRE MARIN
C. D. LEWIS · THE GRAVEYARD BY THE SEA

French text with an English verse translation by C. Day Lewis.
500 copies on mould-made Magnani paper.
Set in 16-point Vicenza italic. 24 pages. 23 × 15 cm.
Printed for Martin Secker & Warburg, London. Verona, September 1946. (70)
Blue, red and yellow marbled paper with label on the upper cover.
   Copy No. 500.   Cup.510.ee.16

42

TAMMARO DE MARINIS
LA BIBLIOTECA NAPOLETANA DEI RE D'ARAGONA · *Volume II*

Italian text. Catalogue of the manuscripts in the former library of the Aragonese Kings at Naples, compiled on the basis of the volumes preserved in the libraries of Europe and America. With a foreword, the inventories made in the fifteenth century, 971 extracts from documents in the Neapolitan archives (destroyed during the war in 1944), a bibliography and indices.
200 copies on hand-made Magnani paper, with 17 reproductions in the text (of which eight engravings were printed on the hand press) and 22 collotype plates printed by Fratelli Alinari, Florence.
Set in 11-, 12- and 14-point Baskerville. xiv+ 378 pages. 38 × 28 cm.
Printed for Ulrico Hoepli, Milan. Verona (1943–1947), January 1947. (71)
Yellow cloth, two dark red labels on spine, top edge gilt, brown and yellow headbands. By Torriani, Milan. (Exhibited copy rebound.)   L.R.301.i.1

Volumes I, III and IV were not published until 1952.

This catalogue of a great Renaissance collection of manuscripts, reconstructed from the surviving volumes dispersed in various libraries, presented a formidable and complex task to the printer. Mardersteig is on record as saying that it went to the limits of the capacity of his hand press.

Alphonso V, the Magnanimous, reigned in Naples from 1443 to 1458. One of the first acts of his reign was to found a royal library of manuscripts rich in the work of contemporary humanist authors and scribes. The formation, growth and dispersal of this library is the subject of this monumental catalogue by Tammaro De Marinis. The successful organization of a profusion of illustrations and appendices, the complex, sober and subtle design, and the precision of the presswork make these volumes a typographical masterpiece.

Volumes I and II, containing the text, were printed at the Officina Bodoni in 1952 and 1947 respectively.

Vol. I contains previous lists, catalogues, inventories and other documents concerning the royal library, facsimiles of scribes' hands and signatures and armorial identifications; then follows a catalogue of the manuscripts.

Vol. II contains a general introduction and a series of chapters devoted to each sovereign as well as chapters on arms, mottoes, miniatures, bindings and on the management of the library. All the documentary evidence is reprinted and surrounded by hundreds of notes which provide an exhaustive source of information about intellectual life in Naples in the fifteenth century. The eventual removal from 1495 onwards of large sections of this library to France and Spain was of great importance in the diffusion of humanism in Europe.

The Stamperia Valdonega

'After the war I believed that the time for expensive books from a hand press had passed. I thought it logical to return to a small machine-printing house of good quality . . . but by myself I would not have been able to maintain such a printing-house in addition to my normal occupation'. With Walter Leonhard Mardersteig established the Stamperia Valdonega in 1948, named after the valley in which it is situated. The backbone of the enterprise were the 8,000 sets of the 86-volume collection of Italian literary texts *La letteratura italiana: storia e testi*, published by Riccardo Ricciardi. Scientific and scholarly texts which required unusually careful setting are still a speciality.

43

Ovid's Metamorphoses: in fifteen books. Translated into English verse under the direction of Sir Samuel Garth by John Dryden, Alexander Pope, Joseph Addison, William Congreve and other eminent hands.

Etchings by Hans Erni. Set in Centaur.
1,500 copies printed by the Stamperia Valdonega. Printed for the members of the Limited Editions Club at the Officina Bodoni in Verona. New York, 1958.

Cup.510.ee.41

The Limited Editions Club of New York was founded in 1929 by George Macy to provide its 1,500 members with editions designed and illustrated by leading typographers and artists.

44

VIRGILIO · LE GEORGICHE

New Italian verse translation of Virgil's *Georgics* with a Note by Giulio Caprin.
Illustrated with twenty etchings by the sculptor Giacomo Manzù.
165 copies on Fabriano mould-made paper, of which the first 20 contain a second suite of the etchings with 10 studies and variants.
Set in 16-point Garamond. 126 pages. 38.5×28 cm.
Printed for Ulrico Hoepli, Milan. Verona, January 1948. (76)
Green goatskin, gold-tooled ears of corn on both covers, green and yellow headbands, black leather doublures. Bound in England.   Copy No. 122.   c.128.k.17

45

ANDRÉ GIDE · THESEUS

English translation by John Russell. Illustrated with twelve lithographs, of which
one is in two colours, and one vignette on the title-page, by Massimo Campigli.
200 copies; 10 on mould-made Fabriano paper and 190 on Magnani paper; the first
30 copies contain a second suite of 12 lithographs and 8 studies printed on
China paper.
Set in 16-point Garamond roman. 104 pages. 33 × 24.5 cm.
Printed for New Directions, Norfolk, Connecticut and G. Heywood Hill, London.
Verona, January 1949. (85)
White paper covers with author and title printed on upper cover and spine.

Copy No. 149.   Loan

Zeno

'After the outcome of the Griffo type, in which we had to reinterpret an already
existing and masterly type-alphabet in order to adapt it to our purpose, I had the
Zeno type cut by Malin. It was intended for the printing of a missal and inspired by
the noble handwritten roman letter of Lodovico degli Arrighi', i.e. in a missal copied
by Arrighi c. 1520 when he was a scribe in the Roman Curia, for Cardinal Giulio
de' Medici, later Pope Clement VII. 'The task of deriving a printing type from a
manuscript letter is more difficult than one would expect and requires great self-
sacrifice, for a type must renounce all personal character and be inconspicuously at
the disposal of the public'.

Mardersteig found it was first necessary to redraw the letters and by eliminating
various characteristic features of the pen to transform the calligraphic letters into a
form more suitable for printing. Charles Malin cut the punches in 1935–36.

The Zeno type, named after Verona's patron saint, first appeared in 1937 in Lorenzo
Montano's stories of the life and miracles of San Zeno, of which an English version
(also set in Zeno) was issued in 1949. Revisions were made in this face; a second state
was shown in *The Gospels* (1962). The projected Officina Bodoni missal was not printed.

46

LORENZO MONTANO · BISHOP SAN ZENO · *Patron of Verona.*

English translation of the Italian text on the life and miracles of San Zeno, patron saint of Verona, published in June 1937 as the first specimen of the new type-face Zeno. Illustrated with three woodcuts by Gunter Böhmer after the statue of the saint (title-page) and the reliefs of the miracles of the saint on the bronze doors of the Basilica of San Zeno, Verona.
60 copies on mould-made Fabriano paper.
Set in 16-point Zeno. 18 pages. 27 × 18 cm.
Editiones Officinae Bodoni: Verona, June 1949. (88)
Brown paper boards with paper labels printed in red on spine and upper cover, top edge gilt, white silk headbands.   Cup.510.ee.18

47

ROBERT BURNS · LIEDER

A selection of the Scottish poet's songs, with the Swiss-German translation in verse facing the original text, a preface by August Corrodi and a postscript by Georg Reinhart. New edition of the text and translation published at Winterthur in 1870.
100 copies on mould-made Fabriano paper.
Set in 11-point Bembo roman and italic. 124 pages. 20 × 13 cm.
Private edition. Verona, September 1949. (89)
Brown pig-skin with blind lines, six raised bands, top edge gilt, scarlet headbands.
                              Copy No. 89.   Cup.510.ee.19

48

DYLAN THOMAS · TWENTY-SIX POEMS

English text. 26 poems selected by the author for this edition.
150 copies signed by the poet: 10 on Japanese vellum, 140 on mould-made Fabriano paper.
Set in 16-point Griffo roman. 78 pages. 30 × 20 cm.
Printed for James Laughlin, Norfolk, Connecticut, and J. M. Dent & Sons, London. Verona, December 1949. (90)
Green and black patterned paper boards, natural cloth spine with paper label, yellow headbands.   Copy No. 44. Cup.510.ee.20

– Another copy.   Copy No. 147.   Loan
Inscribed by the poet to Vernon Watkins 'With Gower love from Dylan'.

This volume of poems by Dylan Thomas was printed in Griffo type by Hans Mardersteig on the hand-press of the Officina Bodoni in Verona for James Laughlin and J. M. Dent & Sons, Ltd. The edition consists of ten copies on Japanese vellum, numbered I to X, and 140 copies on Fabriano hand-made paper, numbered 11 to 150, of which numbers 11 to 60 are for sale in Great Britain, all signed by the author.
December Mcmxxxxix

with fower love from
Dylan.

Dylan Thomas, *Twenty-six Poems* (1949). Colophon. Set in Griffo. (48)

49

TAMMARO DE MARINIS
LA BIBLIOTECA NAPOLETANA DEI RE D'ARAGONA · *Volume I*

Italian text. The story of the library of the Aragonese Kings of Naples in the fifteenth century, its formation, growth and dispersal; including the activities of humanists, calligraphers, miniaturists, bookbinders and librarians at the Neapolitan court. 69 illustrations in the text, mostly in heliogravure. The 69 collotype plates of manuscripts, miniatures and bindings, and the seven facsimiles of documents were printed by Fratelli Alinari, Florence.
200 copies on hand-made Magnani paper.
Set in various sizes of Baskerville. xii + 320 pages. 38 × 28 cm.
Printed for Ulrico Hoepli, Milan. Verona (1950–1952), August 1952. (96)
Binding as for Vol. II (1947). (Exhibited copy rebound.)   L.R.301.i.1

Of Volumes III and IV, also published in 1952, which contain 320 collotype plates, the Officina Bodoni printed the title-pages, the heliogravure vignettes and the indices.

50

BOCCACCIO · THE NYMPHS OF FIESOLE

With woodcuts made by Bartolomeo di Giovanni for a lost Quattrocento edition which were used to illustrate later texts and have now been reassembled and recut.

English prose translation of Boccaccio's poem, made by John Goubourne (based on the French version of 1556 by Antoine Guercin du Crest). Text edited by R. H. Boothroyd after the only known copy of the only edition of this translation, published in London in 1597; with a postscript by Hans Mardersteig and a reproduction in heliogravure of the title-page of the original edition. Illustrated with 23 woodcuts attributed to Bartolomeo di Giovanni and recut by Fritz Kredel. 225 copies on hand-made Fabriano paper. The text set in 16-point Griffo, second state, the postscript in 13-point Bembo. 130 pages. 28 × 19 cm.
Editiones Officinae Bodoni: Verona (1950–1952), December 1952. (97)
Purple wave-patterned paper boards, vellum spine, gilt line, top edge gilt, white headbands.   Copy No. 129.   Cup.510.ee.21

– Another copy.   Copy No. 188.   Loan

– Another copy.   Copy No. 215.   Loan

When he first decided to attempt a reconstruction of the lost fifteenth-century edition of the *Ninfale fiesolano* it was also Mardersteig's intention to reprint not only Boccaccio's original text, but also an English translation. Following a reference to the only English translation he could discover, he eventually found the unique copy of John Goubourne's *A famous tragicall discourse of two lovers, Affrican and Mensola* (1597) in the library of Worcester College, Oxford.

Most of the text of this edition had been set by the summer of 1939, but work was interrupted by the outbreak of war. In February 1940 the Italian text was issued, printed in Bembo italic and with twenty-two of the woodcuts. Before work was resumed on the English version Mardersteig decided to alter his original layout and choice of type.

Mardersteig's postscript or epilogue is the first of such extended notes by the printer which have since appeared in many Officina Bodoni editions.

Boccaccio's poem *Il Ninfale fiesolano* (1939) was the first of several Officina Bodoni books illustrated by early woodcuts. The impressions, however, were printed from blocks cut by modern craftsmen following the early designs. The designs, photographically transferred on to blocks of pearwood, have been reinterpreted through the engraver's hand and eye. The resulting illustrations therefore have the strength and freshness of a true impression, which cannot be obtained by the usual photomechanical methods of reproducing early woodcuts, i.e. by lightly retouching a photographic reproduction of the original pages which were themselves often poorly inked.

the chace, taught them meanes to assaile and vanquish the cruell fiercenes of the beast: called each to recount theyr prayes gotten, at least such as were worthy; praysed those that had doone best, to increase their desire to doo better, and by good and milde exhortations, incited the minds of others to the like.

After many dayes thus spent in devising with her Nymphes, Diana before she departed, elected one whom she made mistres and governesse of the rest, and under paine of her high displeasure, she commanded (as herselfe) to obey in her absence: which commandement was as religiously kept as the nunnes at this day obey their abbesse in what soever she commaundeth. Now were these virgins clothed in white garments, a collour propper to signifie their puritie, antl might thereby easily be knowne. For this cause also of strangers, they were reputed sacred and holy,

12

and to sight so precious, that men doubted to touch them (as fire) for feare of death.

CHAPTER III

How Diana came into the forrest of Flossolan to visite her votaries, and what instructions she gave them neere to the fountaine.

After Diana had spent many dayes with her Nymphes on the Olympian mountaines and confines of Arabia, she determined to returne to Tuscane: and at the first entrie of the flourishing month of May, she approched the forrest of Flossolan, the same beeing the season of the Spring, so sweet and pleasant, that hardly could men see tree, hedge, or grove, uncovered with all sorts of little birds, disclosing with open throates their newe amours. The nightingale warbling her notes with sweet harmonie, accused the disloyaltie of Tirreus. The lynnet with many other small birds, in theyr wood-like tunes, shewed forth the high praises of Venus, from whom the mountaines of joy had taken their grene chaplets, the greene trees theyr new ornaments, and the little hils theyr accustomed deckings: overlooking the valleys and fields with such delight, that each thing seemed to laugh for the pleasantnes of the time. This was also the season, wherein youth of each sexe most felt the hote and amorous vapour of Venus, and the sharpe pricks of the little God Cupid.

13

Boccaccio, *The Nymphs of Fiesole* (1952). Set in Griffo, second state. (50)

Shortly before the engraver Fritz Kredel emigrated to America in 1938 he visited Mardersteig in Verona. Kredel shared his enthusiasm for early woodcuts and Mardersteig admired Kredel's outstanding skill: 'Like the woodcarvers in the days of incunabula he uses a small knife and with admirable accuracy and speed engraves the most delicate lines and drawings on blocks of pearwood . . . I asked him if he would care to make a recut of the illustration used in one of the less accessible works'.

The experiment was successful and so they proceeded with Mardersteig's plan to recut a series of woodcut illustrations from a rare fifteenth-century edition. Mardersteig explains how he came to choose the cuts made by Bartolomeo di Giovanni, a pupil and collaborator of the painter Domenico Ghirlandaio, for an early but lost edition of Boccaccio's poem: 'I consulted Tammaro De Marinis, as I wanted to find not only illustrations, but also a suitable text which would still appeal to modern readers. De Marinis produced from his library a copy of the 1568 edition of Boccaccio's *Ninfale fiesolano* containing sixteen woodcuts [i.e. of a lost fifteenth-century edition] known to us only through this reprint . . . I came to the conclusion that not all the illustrations of the lost original edition had been included in the reprint. By pure

Woodcut by Bartolomeo di Giovanni recut by Fritz Kredel for *The Nymphs of Fiesole* (1952). (50)

chance I saw exhibited in one of the showcases at the Biblioteca Nazionale in Florence a book opened at a page containing a woodcut which could be recognised at first glance as one of the missing *Ninfale* woodcuts, its connection with the text in which it appeared being very vague ... To the sixteen woodcuts of the 1568 edition I was gradually able to add seven others which I found scattered among various reprints, usually of legends of the Saints in verse'.

They were all transferred photographically on to blocks of wood and recut by Kredel. 'Parts which had been damaged or broken off on the original blocks', Mardersteig adds, 'were restored to their pristine clarity'.

51

IL LIBRO DI TOBIA

Italian translation of the Book of Tobit, with 10 engravings on bronze by Dario Viterbo, printed on the copper-plate press.
120 copies on mould-made Fabriano paper.
Set in 20-point Garamond roman. 64 pages. 38.5 × 28 cm.
Printed for the Cento Amici del Libro, Florence. Verona, December 1952. (98)
Dark grey paper boards, title on upper cover, fawn and white headbands.

Cup.502.f.14

52

PUBLII OVIDII NASONIS HEROIDES

Latin text of the fifteen epistles, edited by Luigi Castiglioni. Illustrated with
fifteen full-page lithographs by Francesco Messina printed in dark brown.
166 copies on mould-made Fabriano paper signed by the artist.
Set in 16-point Garamond roman. 138 pages. 38.5 × 28 cm.
Printed for the Istituto di Biblioteconomia e Bibliografia 'Ulrico Hoepli'
dell'Università degli Studi di Milano. Verona, October 1953. (99)
Unbound set of folded quires in original loose paper covers with printed title

Copy No. 85.   Loan

The press-men who printed the book are named in the colophon which is unusual.

53

SERMO DOMINI IN MONTE

The Vulgate text of the Sermon on the Mount (St Matthew, chapters 5–7).
200 copies on mould-made Fabriano paper: 100 copies with the Latin text followed
by the Italian translation of Monsignor Antonio Martini (1769); 50 copies with
the French translation of Canon Crampon; and 50 copies with the Dutch
translation of the Société Petrus Canisius.
Set in 16- and 14-point Zeno. 36 pages. 30 × 20 cm.
Editiones Officinae Bodoni: Verona, December 1953. (100)
Dark brown antique laid paper boards, solid device on upper cover, vellum spine.
Top edge gilt, scarlet headbands.　　　　　Copy No. 9.   Loan

This book was printed for exhibition at the Plantin-Moretus Museum, Antwerp.

54

MARCEL DE GUÉRIN · POÈMES EN PROSE
Les Bruits de la nature, Le Centaure, La Bacchante.

French text.
120 copies: 15 on Japanese vellum, 105 on mould-made Fabriano paper.
Set in 16-point Griffo, second state, the titles in 20-point and 24-point Pacioli.
60 pages. 25 × 16 cm.
Editiones Officinae Bodoni: Verona, January 1954. (101)
Green goatskin, open device in gold on upper cover, top edge gilt, red headbands,
pale grey watered silk ends.　　　　　Copy No. 8.   Loan

One of fifteen copies printed on Japanese vellum is exhibited, with the original paper covers bound in, of which the upper cover has an etching by Renzo Sommaruga printed in black.

The text of *Les Bruits de la nature* had been used for a trial setting in Bodoni types in 1923 of which only four or five copies were printed.

Dante

Mardersteig's third type design called Dante, first used to print Boccaccio's *Trattatello in laude di Dante* (1955), was cut by Charles Malin between 1947 and 1954. Dante roman has a resemblance to Bembo; Dante italic also derives from Francesco Griffo, and is considered to be a more successful companion face for its roman than was the case with Griffo italic. Dante has a related display or titling face, Pacioli, based on the geometrically constructed letters of Fra Luca de Pacioli, whose *De divina proportione* (1509) was printed by the Officina Bodoni in 1956.

Dante was in Morison's view suitable for general book work as well as for printing the hand-set and hand-printed limited editions for which it was designed. He recommended that permission be sought to cut a Monotype version to be made generally available – an unusual distinction for a private press type-face. Between 1957 and 1959 a range of sizes for machine composition was issued by Monotype developed from the original 10- and 12-point sizes.

With Dante, Charles Malin in Mardersteig's view reached the height of his skill as a punch-cutter; it was his greatest achievement, a task he managed to complete shortly before his death in 1956. 'When the inventive powers of Malin came to an end', wrote Mardersteig, 'so did my pleasure in type designing'.

55

BOCCACCIO · TRATTATELLO IN LAUDE DI DANTE

Italian text of Boccaccio's treatise on the life of Dante, based on the transcription by Giovanni Muzzioli of the autograph manuscript in the Capitular Library, Toledo. Critical note by Alfredo Schiaffini. With a reproduction of a hitherto unpublished portrait of Dante from a manuscript in the Biblioteca Capitolare, Verona, and a reproduction in heliogravure of a page of the autograph manuscript. 140 copies; initials printed in red and blue: 15 copies printed on Japanese vellum and 125 on hand-made paper of the Papeteries Rives.

The first appearance of the type-face called Dante designed by Mardersteig and engraved by Charles Malin: set in 12- and 10-point. 130 pages. 21.5 × 13.5 cm.
Editiones Officinae Bodoni: Verona, Autumn 1955. (103) **105**
Red goatskin with open device in gold on the upper cover, blind lines, five raised bands, red leather joints. Top edge gilt, yellow and red headbands.

Copy No. 18. Cup.510.ee.22

– Another copy.

Copy No. 122. Loan

SOLONE, IL CUI PECTO UNO HUMANO TEMPIO DI DIVINA SAPIENTIA FU REPUTATO, E le cui sacratissime leggi sono ancora alli presenti huomini chiara testimoniança della antica giustitia, era, secondo che dicono alcuni, spesse volte usato di dire ogni republica, sì come noi, andare e stare sopra due piedi; de' quali, con matura gravità, affermava essere il destro il non lasciare alcuno difecto commesso impunito, e il sinistro ogni ben facto remunerare. Adgiugnendo che, qualumque delle due cose già dette per vitio o per nigligentia si sottraeva, o meno che bene si servava, sença niuno dubbio quella republica, che 'l faceva, convenire andare scianchata; e se per isciagura si pecchasse in amendue, quasi certissimo avea quella non potere stare in alcun modo.

Mossi adumque più così egregii come antichi popoli da questa laudevole sententia e apertissimamente vera, alcuna volta di deità, altra di marmorea statua, e sovente di celebre sepultura, e tal fiata di triumphale arco, e quando di laurea corona secondo i meriti precedenti honoravano i valorosi; le pene, per opposito, a' colpevoli date non curo di

7

Fra Luca de Pacioli

The Franciscan friar Luca Pacioli was born *c.* 1445 in Borgo San Sepolcro and was famous in his own time as a mathematician. His *Summa de arithmetica, geometria, proportione etc.* (1494), is a mathematical encyclopaedia, the first of its kind to be printed. It contains, among other things, an early example of the calculus of probability, a calculated logarithm (at least a century before Napier) and important sections on double-entry book-keeping and algebra. Between 1496 and 1499 Pacioli was one of the group of scientists and artists at the court of Lodovico Sforza 'il Moro', Duke of Milan, among whom the most outstanding was Leonardo da Vinci. Pacioli later taught in various universities, and in 1509 in Venice published his *De divina proportione*.

Vitruvius, the ancient Roman writer on architecture, in his *De architectura*, bk. III, ch. 1, describes, as proof of the harmony and perfection of the human body, how a well-built man, with outstretched hands and feet fits exactly into those perfect geometrical figures, the circle and the square.

In the course of Pacioli's *De divina proportione* Vitruvius' concept is given a metaphysical significance: 'First we shall talk of the proportions of man, because from the human body derive all measures and their names, and in it is to be found every ratio and proportion by which God reveals the innermost secrets of nature'. The ancients proportioned all their work, particularly temples, in accordance with the human body. 'For in the human body they found the two main figures without which it is impossible to achieve anything, namely the perfect circle . . . and the square'.

For Pacioli these proportions are inherent also in the perfect capital letter, to be found in the letters of Roman inscriptions and in the formal script based on them, the *lettera antica formata*. Felice Feliciano's procedures for constructing Roman capitals were adopted by Pacioli and appended to his *De divina proportione*.

56

LUCA PACIOLI · DE DIVINA PROPORTIONE

Italian text edited by Franco Riva from a manuscript in the Ambrosian Library, Milan. With a note by G. Masotti-Biggiogero.
60 colour plates from the 'Corpi regolari' drawn by Leonardo da Vinci, two in heliogravure and two facsimiles; the plates were printed by A. Belli, Milan.
280 copies printed in black and red on mould-made Magnani paper.

Set in 16-point 'Monotype' Bembo, leaded 2 points; the titles in 18-, 24- and
30-point Pacioli. xxx+ 250 pages. 28 × 20 cm.
Printed for the Mediobanca di Milano. Verona, December 1956. **106**
Fontes ambrosianae vol. xxxi.
Brown cloth, geometrical drawing blocked in gold on upper cover, brown
goatskin spine with gold line, top edge gilt, brown and yellow headbands.

Copy No. 36.   C.103.g.31

– Another copy. Copy No. 39.
Lent by the Syndics of the Cambridge University Library.

The proportion which Pacioli calls 'divine' is that now usually known as the Golden
Section, by which a line is divided in such a way that the shorter part is to the longer
as the longer is to the whole line. 'The whole is to the largest part as the largest part
is to the smaller' (Euclid, II, 11). By extension the Golden Rectangle is one of the
most aesthetically satisfying of all geometrical figures.

This ratio also occurs in the theory of regular polygons and polyhedra. Pacioli, among
his examples drawn from the sciences and the arts in which the beauty of the 'divine
proportion' is to be seen, adduces these geometrical figures. The sixty drawings of
regular bodies, here reproduced for the first time in colour from the Ambrosian
manuscript, were, as Pacioli tells us, 'made and shaped by that ineffable left hand
most fitted for all the mathematical disciplines of the prince among mortals of today,
that first of Florentines, our Leonardo da Vinci, in that happy time when we were
together in . . . Milan, working for the same patron'. Drawings of some of the same
figures are also to be found in Leonardo's Atlantic Codex. Pacioli himself drew a
number of diagrams in the margins of his text which are also reproduced in the
Officina Bodoni edition.

The first of the three parts of Pacioli's book is the *Compendium de divina proportione*,
which contains the illustrations of solid geometry by Leonardo. Pacioli detects in the
divine proportion an aesthetic principle which is to be found also in the human body,
in the elements of architecture and in Roman capital letters. These considerations
form the second part of the book. He constructs his letters geometrically with elegant
results. Mardersteig had these letters cut by Charles Malin as a titling fount which
he called Pacioli; it is used on the title-page of this edition. The third part is an Italian
translation – unacknowledged – of a mathematical treatise, *De corporibus regularibus*,
by Pacioli's compatriot and teacher, the painter Piero della Francesca.

The Officina Bodoni edition provides not only fine facsimiles but achieves a new
realization of text and illustration in a masterpiece of clear and balanced typography.

57

EZRA POUND · DIPTYCH ROME–LONDON
Homage to Sextus Propertius & Hugh Selwyn Mauberly. Contacts and Life

English text.
200 copies printed in black and red on mould-made Magnani paper and signed by the author.
Set in 16-point Bembo, roman and italic. 80 pages. 28.5 × 20 cm.
Printed for James Laughlin, New York; Faber & Faber, London; and Vanni Scheiwiller, Milan. Verona, December 1957. **109**

Copy No. 148.   Cup.510.ee.25

– Another copy, to show the binding.   Copy No. 172.   Loan
Old rose paper boards, with EP in gold on upper cover.

58

T. E. LAWRENCE · FROM A LETTER

English text. Part of a letter dated Le Petit Andelys, August 1910 and signed Ned.
60 copies printed on white antique laid paper. 22 × 13 cm. Set in 12-point Dante.
Printed for presentation by the printer to members of the Double Crown Club, London, on 11 June 1959.
Pink Ingres paper, solid device printed in grey on upper cover.   Loan

59

T. S. ELIOT · FOUR QUARTETS

English text.
290 copies printed on mould-made Magnani paper and signed by the author.
Set in 14- and 12-point Dante. 50 pages. 30 × 20.5 cm.
Printed for Faber & Faber, London. Verona, July 1960. **112**
Green, red, yellow ochre and gold marbled paper boards.
Vellum spine, gilt line, top edge gilt, green headbands.

Copy No. 5.   Cup.510.ee.27

– Another copy.   Copy No. 256.   Loan

In the ninth impression (July 1952) of the Faber & Faber edition of *Four Quartets* there was a misplaced break between two sections of 'Burnt Norton'. Although this mistake was corrected by a cancel leaf in half the impression of 10,000 copies, unfortunately Mardersteig was sent one of the incorrect copies to set his type from, and so the final five lines of section IV appear as the first five lines of section V. Eliot, knowing the Officina Bodoni's high reputation, said he had no need to see proofs.

Felice Feliciano (1433–79)

Referring to his longstanding interest in Felice Feliciano Mardersteig wrote: 'In retrospect one often notices with surprise enigmatic links in the course of one's own life. Even before I thought of living in Verona I had started to concern myself with Felice Feliciano, the Veronese author, printer, poet and antiquary, who created the first Renaissance geometric construction of the alphabet using the square and the circle, which Albrecht Dürer later attempted. When I had to move to Verona I was enabled to trace the unexplored life of this humanist'.

Feliciano, by profession a copyist and calligrapher, was an assiduous collector and recorder of ancient inscriptions and called himself 'Antiquarius'. He transcribed a biography of his predecessor in epigraphy, Cyriac of Ancona. He was a friend of the painters Giovanni Bellini, Marco Zoppo and Andrea Mantegna. With Mantegna, to whom he dedicated a collection of inscriptions, and Giovanni Marcanova, a rich physician of Padua, Feliciano made an archaeological field-trip around Lake Garda in 1464, of which he has left a charming account known as his *Jubilatio*.

They met one afternoon with other members of an antiquarian society on the western shore of Lake Garda where they first crowned themselves with myrtle and ivy, and then visited the ruins of a temple of Diana. Afterwards they decorated their boat with laurel and left the shore for the islands. The music of the lyre accompanied them to Sirmione where they visited the church of St Peter to give thanks for a pleasant day. Some twenty-two inscriptions were copied on that day.

Feliciano in later life took up alchemy and learnt printing in Ferrara. He printed one book at Pojano in 1476, an edition in Italian of Petrarch's *De viris illustribus*. The young Felice Feliciano was probably the first scholar to make a thorough study of the shapes of the letters he admired on Roman inscriptions, by going back to the principles of geometrical construction; and the earliest designer of an alphabet after classic models, using the square and the circle. He wrote an explanation of his constructions which survives in a single manuscript, Codex Vat. lat. 6852.

60

FELICE FELICIANO VERONESE · ALPHABETUM ROMANUM
Edited by Giovanni Mardersteig

An edition of Codex Vat. lat. 6852 which contains the treatise by the Veronese
humanist Felice Feliciano on the geometrical construction of Roman capital letters.
English version by R. H. Boothroyd. With an introduction by G. Mardersteig on
the revival of the letter-forms in Roman inscription; on Felice Feliciano and his
alphabet construction.
Illustrations in the text and five heliogravure plates of ancient inscriptions and
initials from manuscripts written by Felice Feliciano. The 25 letters of the alphabet
were coloured by hand by Ameglio Trivella, after the original manuscript.
Set in 12-, 11- and 10-point Dante, roman and italic. 140 pages. 22.5 × 15.5 cm.
400 copies of the English edition printed on Magnani paper of Pescia.
Officina Bodoni: Verona, November 1960. **113**
German and Italian versions were also published in the same year.
Dark brown goatskin, open device blocked in gold on upper cover, five raised
bands, grey-green Ingres paper ends, top edge gilt, yellow and brown headbands.

Copy No. 96.   Loan

– Another copy. Copy No. 154.   Loan

The colophon names the press-men who worked on this edition: 'Set in Giovanni
Mardersteig's Dante type and printed on his hand press in 400 numbered copies by
Mario Facincani and Rino Grazioli'.

Up to 1960, while the choice of texts to be printed usually reflected Mardersteig's
taste, his participation in the productions of the press was confined to carefully
editing the text and to conferring on it a fine typographical form. The importance
Mardersteig attached to this book is shown not only in the unusually large number
of copies printed, but also in the inclusion of his own long essay on aspects of Feliciano's
life and work, much of it the result of his own researches.

Mardersteig in his introduction maintains that the capital letters used in classic
Roman inscriptions are the single most living element in the heritage handed down
to us from antiquity. In the early years of the Roman Empire, he observes, 'their
proportions were so carefully calculated that they could be constructed geometrically
within a square and a circle described inside it. The addition of serifs . . . gave them
a static beauty. The proportion between the chief strokes of these letters and their
height is about 1:10, whereas the width of the lighter strokes is one half or a third
of that of the chief strokes'.

It is probably from the Roman writer on architecture, Vitruvius, that Feliciano
derived the idea of the perfection of the number ten. Vitruvius showed that the
human body may be divided longitudinally into ten units, each of which is equal to
the face from the chin to the top of the forehead. Moreover, the perfect forms of

circle and square were also applicable to the human body. Feliciano's constructions of Roman capital letters in the Vatican manuscript are based on these Vitruvian principles.

According to his own statement Feliciano rediscovered the principles of geometrical construction: 'It was an old usage to form the letter from a circle and square ... And this is what I, Felice Feliciano, found in old letters by making measurements ... both in the noble city of Rome and other places'.

Felice Feliciano's treatise on the alphabet is preserved in a single autograph manuscript, Codex Vat. lat. 6852, which Mardersteig dates, from the style of other autographs, as not later than 1460. It is the first treatise to show in theory and practice how Roman capitals modelled on those of ancient inscriptions should be formed. Codex Vat. lat. 6852 was discovered by the historian Theodor Mommsen, and edited and published by Rudolf Schöne in 1874. Written on both sides of seventeen vellum sheets, the first 25 pages contain drawings of each letter of the alphabet with directions for its construction below. These are followed by Feliciano's treatise, his recipes for making ink, and an epigram by Paolo Ramusio.

The drawn letters contain internal sepia lines and are shaded in combinations of two colours to indicate how they are to be drawn or cut, though this gives them the appearance of standing up in relief, i.e. they are apparently faceted or prismatic, the reverse of incised letters. The constructional dots, circles, squares and diagonals are drawn faintly in diluted ink so as not to impair the effect of the finished letters.

In the Officina Bodoni edition the letters have been redrawn (and slightly reduced) for printing, and hand-tinted in the colours of the original. Each letter is printed on a right-hand page with the Italian text below. A diagram of its geometric construction is printed on the facing page; these diagrams have been redrawn not only from the dots, circles and lines still visible in the manuscript but also following Feliciano's own prescriptions in the text. 'The width of the chief stroke should be one tenth of the height', he wrote. The proportions prescribed by later designers of letters vary between 1:12 (Damianus Moyllus and Leon Battista Alberti) and 1:9 (Luca de Pacioli). The 1:10 proportion, which stems from Vitruvius, corresponds closely to that of a number of Augustan inscriptions, though the letters on the base of Trajan's column (AD 113) observe Alberti's norm of 1:12. In the *Hypnerotomachia Poliphili* Francesco Colonna mentions 'splendid capitals proportioned as one-to-nine'.

Mardersteig discovered a practical application of Feliciano's alphabet in Verona in two inscriptions dated 5 September 1468, on the round arch and transom of the middle doorway of the Pescheria (the former fish-market), the earliest Renaissance building in the city. These inscriptions correspond in style to the heading of a manuscript of Plato's *Phaedo* written by Feliciano in 1460, and are apparently designed by him.

Feliciano's treatise was followed by others which gave methods for constructions based mainly upon their predecessors, notably those of Damianus Moyllus (*c.* 1480), of Luca de Pacioli (1509) and of Torniello (1517), which have all been reprinted by the Officina Bodoni, and Dürer's *Unterweysung der Messung* (1525). For all these authors the letters of the alphabet, as well as the human body and architectural forms, derived their beauty from an inherent numerical proportionality – a concept which is objectively verifiable where the harmony of musical sounds is concerned. Feliciano's alphabet is also important, because the geometrical construction of letters subsequently became the basis of the work of a number of type designers.

61

Felice Feliciano: Preface to a volume of autograph copies of his formal epistles in Italian, *c.* 1472. Harley MS. 5271, ff.2b–3

The preface exhibited here, written by Feliciano on three leaves of coloured vellum in gold and silver letters and addressed to a certain Canon Alberto, begins: 'Salve qui legeris memento Feliciani. Candida fulvo nobilior auro facundia Felix'. The author of the preface – ostensibly not Feliciano himself though it is in his hand – cites Valerius Maximus and praises eloquence, of which the epistles of his friend Feliciano are models.

62

HUGH MACDIARMID · THE KIND OF POETRY I WANT

English text, with an introduction and a note by the author.
300 copies on mould-made Magnani paper, signed by the author.
Text set in 16-point Griffo, roman and italic; notes in 13-point. 64 pages.
29×20 cm. **114**
Printed for K. D. Duval, Edinburgh. Verona, July 1961.
Brown patterned paper boards, vellum spine, gilt line, top edge gilt, green
headbands. Copy No. 7. Cup.510.ee.29

63

T. S. ELIOT · THE WASTE LAND

English text, with a note by the poet.
300 copies on mould-made Magnani paper, signed by the author.
Text set in 14- and 12-point Dante, roman and italic; notes in 12-point. 24 pages.
29×20 cm.
Printed for Faber & Faber, London. Verona, December 1961. **115**
Brown, green, yellow ochre and gold marbled paper boards, vellum spine with
gilt line, top edge gilt, green headbands. Copy No. 239. Cup.510.ee.28

– Another copy. Copy No. 202. Loan

in praetorium, congregaverunt ad eum universam cohortem. Et exuentes eum, chlamydem coccineam circumdederunt ei; et plectentes coronam de spinis, posuerunt super caput eius, et arundinem in dextera eius. Et genu flexo ante eum, illudebant ei, di-

centes: Ave, rex Iudaeorum. Et expuentes in eum, acceperunt arundinem, et percutiebant caput eius. Et postquam illuserunt ei, exuerunt eum chlamyde, et induerunt eum vestimentis eius, et duxerunt eum ut crucifigerent. Exeuntes autem invenerunt hominem Cyrenaeum, nomine Simonem; hunc angariaverunt ut tolleret crucem eius. Et venerunt in locum, qui dicitur Golgotha, quod est Calvariae locus. Et dederunt ei vinum bibere cum felle mistum. Et cum gustasset, noluit bibere. Postquam autem

124

64

THE HOLY GOSPEL
ACCORDING TO MATTHEW · MARK · LUKE AND JOHN

English text from the Authorized, or King James, version of the Bible with a woodcut frontispiece engraved by Reynolds Stone and a note by G. Mardersteig. Illustrated with 114 woodcuts by Bartolomeo di Giovanni and recut by Bruno Bramanti from *Epistole & Evangelii & Lectioni vulgari in lingua toschana*, Florence 1495; the last eight were cut after Bramanti's death by his pupil Italo Zetti. 320 copies on hand-made Magnani paper.
Set in 16- and 14-point Zeno, second state. 372 pages. 30.5×20 cm.
Editiones Officinae Bodoni: Verona, July 1962. **117**
Latin and Italian texts of the Gospels were also published in 1963.
Red goatskin, title in ornamental circle blocked in gold on upper cover, grey Ingres paper ends, top edge gilt, red and yellow headbands, red leather joints.

Copy D.   Cup.510.ee.30

– Another copy.

Copy No. xv.   Loan

Epistole et Evangelii (1495), an edition of the epistles and gospels from the Missal, survives in two copies only. It is illustrated by 164 woodcuts showing 142 scenes from the Old and New Testaments and 22 small vignettes with half-length figures of Prophets and Evangelists, the most considerable single achievement of fifteenth-century Florentine book illustration. 'The preliminary designs can be attributed without hesitation to Bartolomeo di Giovanni, though blocks were actually cut by several able artists, whose differing styles and techniques can be distinguished. To this Master Bartolomeo, truly a born illustrator and one of the most important and fertile of his time, may be attributed most of the woodcut illustrations made in Florence between about 1490 and the first ten years of the sixteenth century . . . In the present edition we have limited ourselves to the reproduction of the 114 Gospel woodcuts'.

65

EUGENIO MONTALE · OSSI DI SEPPIA

Italian text of an early poem of Montale, who was awarded a Nobel Prize for literature in 1976.
Printed in black and red. 104 pages. 28.5 × 19.5 cm.
165 copies on mould-made Magnani paper, signed by the author.
Set in 14-point Dante, roman and italic.
Editiones Officinae Bodoni: Verona, October 1964. **124**
Mulberry patterned paper boards, vellum spine with gilt line, top edge gilt, dark mulberry headbands.   Copy No. 123.   Cup. 510.ee.31

66

FRANCISCI PETRARCAE ASCENSUS MONTIS VENTOSI & JEAN-HENRI FABRE UNE ASCENSION AU MONT VENTOUX

Latin text of Petrarch's letter and Italian translation by Enrico Bianchi; French text of J.-H. Fabre's essay. With notes by Giuseppe Billanovich on Petrarch's account of his ascent of Mont Ventoux, and by G. Mardersteig on J.-H. Fabre.
175 copies printed on Cernobbio paper. 86 pages. 24.5 × 15.5 cm.
Set in 14-, 12- and 8-point Dante, roman and italic.
Editiones Officinae Bodoni: Verona, March 1965. **125**
Vellum-coloured Linson boards, open device in gold on upper cover, top edge gilt, green headbands.   *Ad personam.*   Loan

– Another copy.   *Ad personam.*   Loan

The 75 *ad personam* copies were presented to the recipients by the printer by way of thanks for their good wishes on the occasion of his seventieth birthday.

67

GUIDO CAVALCANTI · LE RIME

Italian text of the sonnets, *ballate* and *canzoni* of Cavalcanti (*c.* 1255–1300), edited
with an essay by Gianfranco Contini.
On the frontispiece the family tree of the Cavalcanti family.
165 copies printed in red and black on mould-made Fabriano paper; also six copies
printed on vellum and four on Japanese vellum. 114 pages. 21.5×13.5 cm.
Poems set in 16-point Arrighi 'Vicentino' and the essay in 12-point Centaur and Arrighi
italic. Red initials in 24-point Centaur.
Editiones Officinae Bodoni: Verona, February 1966. **130**
Vellum boards, open device in gold on upper cover, top edge gilt, red headbands.
Copy No. 118.   Loan

68

EZRA POUND'S CAVALCANTI POEMS

English versions by Ezra Pound of Cavalcanti's poems with an introduction and
three essays by Pound. On the frontispiece the family tree of the Cavalcanti family.
200 copies, of which 190 were printed on hand-made Magnani paper and ten on
Japanese vellum, all signed by the author. 108 pages. 29×19 cm.
Poems set in 14-point Dante italic with initials in 36-point. Prose in 12-point Dante,
roman and italic.
Printed for 'New Directions', New York; Faber & Faber, London; and Vanni
Scheiwiller, Milan; and the Officina Bodoni, Verona, May 1966. **132**
Yellow antique laid paper boards, with EP blocked in gold on upper cover, vellum
spine, top edge gilt, yellow and red headbands.   Copy No. 134.   Loan

69

ERACLITO · *I frammenti di una perduta opera sulla natura seguiti dalle
testimonianze di vari autori antichi.*

The fragments of a lost work of Heraclitus of Ephesus in an Italian version by
Carlo Diano. Seven of the fragments in Greek printed on a red ground from
blocks designed by G. Mardersteig. With 61 'Testimonianze', or quotations from
ancient authors about Heraclitus and his teaching, in Italian.
150 copies on mould-made Magnani paper. 66 pages. 39.5×28.5 cm.
Italian text set in 20- and 16-point Garamond; the Greek text in Griffo Greek
capitals.
Printed for Enrico Augeri, Milan. Verona, June 1966. **134**
Black paper boards, vellum spine with gilt line, yellow headbands.
Copy No. 78.   L.R.420.CC.22

70

GIOVANNI MARDERSTEIG · *An account of his work by John Dreyfus*

English text of an address by John Dreyfus given at Gallery 303, New York, with type specimens.
135 copies on mould-made Magnani paper. 32 pages. 23 × 15 cm.
Set in 11-point Dante roman; the specimens of Griffo and Zeno in 16-point, of Dante in 14-point, and Pacioli in 30-point.
Keepsake printed for Gallery 303, New York. Verona, October 1966. **135**
Light grey Ingres paper, open device printed in red on upper cover. Loan

71

ΕΠΙΚΤΗΤΟΣ · MANUALE DI EPITETTO
con PAGINE DELLO STESSO DALLE DIATRIBE

Latin and Italian texts: I. the *Enchiridion* of Epictetus translated by Giacomo Leopardi; II. the passages from the *Diatribes* selected and translated by Vittorio Enzo Alfieri; III. the *Enchiridion* in the Latin version of Angelo Poliziano. Note by Giovanni Mardersteig.
160 copies on Cernobbio paper; five copies also printed on Japanese vellum.
Set in 16- and 12-point Centaur and Arrighi italic. 200 pages. 25 × 15.5 cm.
Editiones Officinae Bodoni: Verona, August 1967. **137**
Light blue quarter goatskin with open device in gold on upper cover, top edge gilt. Copy No. 148. Loan

The *Enchiridion* of Epictetus (c. AD 55–135), the most important document of Stoicism under the Roman Empire, was written by the historian Arrian, a pupil of Epictetus, as a guide to his philosophy.

72

LEONARD BASKIN · TO COLOUR THOUGHT

English text with ten illustrations printed by the Meriden Gravure Co., Connecticut. The frontispiece is a reproduction from William Blake's *Small Book of Designs*.
300 copies printed on Cernobbio paper in red and black.
Set in 12-, 11-, and 10-point Dante. 32 pages. 24 × 15.5 cm.
Printed for the Beinecke Library, New Haven, Connecticut. Verona, September 1967. **138**
Light brown antique laid paper boards, brown goatskin spine, top edge gilt, green headbands. Copy No. 140. Loan

For this book the paper was sent first to America for the printing of the illustrations because the originals were there. The sheets were then returned to Verona where the printing of the text and the binding were carried out.

The lettering on the spines of Officina Bodoni books usually reads upwards from tail to head. At the publisher's request, however, the title was sometimes lettered from head to tail, as in this instance.

73

Giovanni Mardersteig: *The Remarkable Story of a Book made in Padua in 1477. Gentile da Foligno's commentary on Avicenna printed by Petrus Maufer.*
Translated by Hans Schmoller.
Nattali & Maurice: London. Set and printed at the Stamperia Valdonega, 1967.

2704.bl.14

Mardersteig's monograph on the printing and publishing of Petrus Maufer's *Avicenna* at Padua in 1477, a story reconstructed from contemporary archives on an almost day-by-day basis, is possibly the most complete account there is of the making of any incunable.

74

ALEXANDER PUSHKIN · IL CAVALIERE DI BRONZO
Racconto Pietroburghese · 1833

Russian text opposite the Italian verse translation by Nerina Martini Bernardi.
165 copies printed in red and black on mould-made Magnani paper.
Russian text set in 14-point Puškin, the Cyrillic type designed by Wadim Lazursky, in the second cutting made for this edition by Ruggero Olivieri; Italian text in 14-point Dante. All copies are signed by the designers of the two types.
On the frontispiece a framed vignette of the monument of Peter the Great.
62 pages. 29×19.5 cm.
Editiones Officinae Bodoni: Verona, January 1968. **141**
Indian red and black patterned paper boards, vellum spine with gilt line, top edge gilt, red headbands.

Copy No. 64.　Cup.510.ee.43

75

SOPHOCLES · KING OEDIPUS

English text in the translation of E. Watling, with seven etchings by Giacomo Manzù. The colophon signed by the artist.

105 copies on mould-made Magnani paper; nine were also printed on Japanese Kaji Torinoko paper.

Set in 16- and 14-point Dante, roman and italic. 100 pages. 38×28 cm.

Printed for Racolin Press Inc., New York. Verona, May 1968. **143**

Loose quires in a vellum-coloured Linson cover with an embossed medallion of the head of Oedipus designed by Manzù; green goatskin spine.

Copy No. 70.   Loan

An Italian edition was also published in the same year.

Giambattista Bodoni's type designs

In 1766, after working for eight years in the printing house of the *Propaganda fide* in Rome, Bodoni set out for England. He was impressed by the volumes he had seen printed by John Baskerville and wanted to widen his professional experience. Bodoni did not reach England. He caught malaria and was forced to stop at Saluzzo, his home town, until he recovered.

At that time the duchy of Parma was being developed by its rulers as a centre for the sciences and the arts. Parma needed its own printing house if it were to follow the examples of the courts of Paris, Madrid and Turin. Bodoni, at the invitation of the ducal librarian whom he had known in Rome, became in 1768 director of the new printing house at Parma which he organized from scratch. For his types he chose those of Pierre-Simon Fournier called *le jeune*, the most recent of a distinguished line of French letter engravers and type-founders, who had just published the two volumes of his *Manuel typographique*. With Fournier's types Bodoni did some printing but his preference was for designing, engraving and casting ornaments and type faces. He obtained permission to set up and run at his own expense a type foundry which he supplied with punches cut by his own hand. The casting was done by his brother, and Bodoni's types were made available to other printers as well as to the ducal printing house.

Mardersteig in the introductory note to his facsimile edition of G. B. Bodoni's *Manuale tipografico, 1788* (1968) summed up Bodoni's style in letter design by his three main innovations. First, Bodoni gave a vertical alignment to the sloped swellings in the bowls of letters which derive from the down-strokes in handwriting. Second, he made all the horizontal serifs on the upper and lower parts of the letters very thin and uniform. Third, he increased the contrast between stems and serifs.

76

GIAMBATTISTA BODONI · MANUALE TIPOGRAFICO 1788
Facsimile a cura di Giovanni Mardersteig.

Introductory note by G. Mardersteig, followed by the preface of Giambattista
Bodoni to his 'Saggio tipografico' of 1771. XLVI + 372 pages. 31 × 23 cm.
The letterpress facsimile is in two parts:
I. the series of roman and italic types, together with specimens of some of the
same letters in the style of Fournier (155 specimens in all).
II. the series of Greek types, some in a second cutting (29 specimens in all).
206 copies on Cernobbio paper; 26 copies printed in memory of Enrico Mattioli
were not for sale. An English version of the introductory note, printed in December
1968 for the Chiswick Bookshop of New York, was inserted in copies no. 101–180.
The introductory note set in 12- and 10-point Bodoni; Bodoni's preface in a
recutting of a fount by Fournier.
Editiones Officinae Bodoni: Verona, November 1968. **144**
Orange-brown stained Linson boards, paper label on spine, green headbands.
                    Copy printed for the British Museum.   L.R.413.h.17

Although it is generally less monumental than the more famous two-volume *Manuale*,
published posthumously in 1818, this rare type specimen illustrates the evolution of
Bodoni's typographic style from his first types, modelled on those of Fournier, to the
184 founts shown.

   Mardersteig's choice of the 1788 edition of the *Manuale* rather than that of 1818, or
the *Fregi e majuscole* of 1771, reflects an accurate judgement of Bodoni's historical
importance. It was not until the 1780s that Bodoni ceased to copy or improve on the
work of Fournier and to develop a typographical style of his own, to be seen in his
vertical stress, fine hair lines and sharply tapered rectangular serifs. The specimen
consists of a series of sentences about Italian towns, one for each size of type, in Italian
for the roman and in French for the italic, ending with 'Saluces ma chère patrie' for
the largest ('*Papale*') size.

   Mardersteig's own text was set in Bodoni types. The facsimile was also printed on
the hand press: an enlarged photographic print was made for each page of Bodoni's
Manuale, which was retouched to produce a rendering of the original letters un-
distorted by the imperfect inking technique of Bodoni's day. Each page was then
reduced to the original size and a line-block made for printing. The facsimile in this
way provides a more accurate rendering of Bodoni's typographical material than the
original edition.

   The roman specimen on fol. 71, missing in all known copies of the *Manuale*, was
supplied from a proof in the Biblioteca Communale at Lugano; the corresponding
italic seems not to have survived.

   Bodoni's first type specimen, *Fregi e majuscole incise e fuse da G. B. Bodoni* (1771) was
modelled on Fournier's manual and printed with borders of type ornament. It con-

tains a preface, which Bodoni's manual of 1788, reproduced in this facsimile edition, lacks. This Preface, addressed by Bodoni to his fellow printers, was included in the Officina Bodoni edition, because it is still useful and instructive.

The 1788 *Manuale* was published in an edition of probably 150 copies, many of which were kept in printing houses as type specimen books. Not many copies have survived. 'For the reproduction of this edition we have made use of several copies from which we have chosen the best printed result'.

Cento, situata
vicino al Fiu-
me Reno, ed è
patria del ce-
leb. Francesco
Barbieri, det-
to il Guercino

Specimen of 'Cento' from facsimile edition of G. B. Bodoni, *Manuale tipografico, 1788.* (76)

77

GIOVANNI MARDERSTEIG · ON G. B. BODONI'S TYPE FACES

English text: 'Giambattista Bodoni and his types used on the hand press of the Officina Bodoni', illustrated with specimens of 12-, 14-, 16- and 20-point Bodoni, followed by 'Specimen pages from Bodoni's *Manuale tipografico 1788*', with examples of letters in the styles of Fournier and Bodoni. 200 copies on hand-made Magnani paper. (50 copies on a different paper were reprinted in 1968.)
Set in Bodoni types. 32 pages. 25×16.5 cm.
Keepsake for Gallery 303, New York. Verona, November 1968. **145**
Paper boards with green Roma antique laid paper wrappers, open device printed on upper cover, and author and title printed in red on spine.   Loan

78

ZACHARIAS FERRERIUS · IN DIE FESTO NATALIS

Latin text of the hymn for Christmas from *Zachariae Ferrerii hymni novi ecclesiastici*, printed by Lodovico degli Arrighi Vicentino and Lautizio Perugino, Rome, 1525.
80 copies printed on hand-made Magnani paper.
Set in 16-point Arrighi 'Vicenza' with calligraphic initials in red from Arrighi's writing book *Il modo di temperare le penne*, Rome, 1523. 28 pages. 9×12 cm.
Private edition for Alberto Falck, and Paul & André Jammes. Verona, 1968.
Vellum-coloured Linson boards, paper label printed in red on spine.   Loan

79

ZACHARIAS FERRERIUS · IN DIE FESTO EPIPHANIAE
Choriambicum alphabeticum.

Latin text of the hymn for Epiphany from *Hymni novi ecclesiastici*, printed by Lodovico degli Arrighi Vicentino and Lautizio Perugino, Rome, 1525.
60 copies printed on hand-made Cernobbio paper.
Set in 16-point Arrighi 'Vicentino' with calligraphic initials in blue from Arrighi's *Il modo di temperare le penne*. 28 pages. 9×12 cm.
Printed by Giovanni Mardersteig for his friends in the USA. Signed by the printer.
Officina Bodoni: Verona, 1968.
Vellum-coloured Linson boards, paper label printed in blue on spine.

Cup.510.ee.37

The future of the hand press

In 1968 Mardersteig saw no easy future for the hand press: 'Difficulties in obtaining the proper materials approach the impossible. The basic materials have changed. Most rags are now of synthetic fibre and cannot be sorted to produce the right mixture for hand-made paper...Hemp, which is an important constituent of good paper is disappearing, because fishing nets and sails, once the most sought-after source, are now made of nylon. Vine-black, that is, soot from burnt vines for the manufacture of deep black printing ink, is no longer available. Good leather for binding can only be obtained with difficulty and after waiting a long time'.

80

CARMI E FAVOLE DEL LAGO DI GARDA

Texts in verse and prose by G. Fracastoro, Pietro Bembo and B. Lenotti.
225 copies printed on hand-made Cernobbio paper. The title-page, half-title and borders in blue.
Set in 12-point Dante roman and italic. 40 pages. 22×14 cm.
Private edition. Dedication 'Per le nozze di Martino e Gabriella', 9 April 1969.
Officina Bodoni: Verona, March 1969.
Vellum-coloured Linson boards with calligraphic initials 'M & G' in gold on upper cover, top edge gilt, blue headbands.   Loan

Francesco Griffo's types

Mardersteig in his note on the types used in his edition of Bembo's *De Aetna*, i.e. Monotype Bembo and his own Griffo type, explains their historical background. 'Connoisseurs of Venetian incunabula . . . generally agree that the roman used by Nicolas Jenson is the most beautiful of all types. At the end of last century a true renaissance of this type took place in England. On the initiative of Emery Walker several recuttings of Jenson's roman were made'. They included William Morris's Golden type and Charles Ricketts' Vale type. The types made for the Doves Press, owned by T. J. Cobden-Sanderson and Emery Walker, were modelled on Jenson's roman, and so too was the type which Walker produced for Count Harry Kessler's Cranach Press and, above all, the Centaur type designed by Bruce Rogers. 'Only the last of these versions can be counted a success', Mardersteig considered.

Admiration for Jenson deflected the attention of typographical reformers from other possible models. 'It was left to Stanley Morison to point out the excellent quality of the type first used by Aldus Manutius in his edition of Bembo's *De Aetna* for which Francesco Griffo had cut the punches. After the not wholly successful revival of the Aldine *Poliphilus* type, Morison, as typographical adviser to The Monotype Corporation, decided that this other Aldine type (later to become universally known as Bembo) should also be recut'.

The type of the 'De Aetna' (1495)

Griffo's lower case was narrower than the round letter forms of Jenson's type and bears less resemblance to handwriting. The finer serifs stand in greater contrast with the weight of the main vertical strokes. The upper case made use of some letters from a set of Greek capitals which Griffo had cut in the previous year for the first

Aldine publication; these letters were supplemented by the specifically roman C D F G L Q R and V. All Griffo's capitals (unlike Jenson's) are shorter than the ascenders b d f h k l; their shapes were influenced by Roman lapidary inscriptions following examples of the revived antique letter forms to be seen on buildings and in paintings.

Francesco Griffo of Bologna

Francesco Griffo, the son of a goldsmith, was born in Bologna *c*. 1450 and followed his father's trade. Like some other goldsmiths Griffo turned to cutting punches for types. He supplied printers in Padua and then in Venice with his founts.

Between 1494 and 1501 he cut the types used by the scholar-printer Aldus Manutius. These included, as well as the *De Aetna* type, the first italic, i.e. types modelled on the sloped cursive handwriting of the period which were Griffo's invention. Mardersteig suggests that the technique of typecasting was not then sufficiently advanced to cope with the exceptionally fine serifs on Griffo's *De Aetna* letters. 'Perhaps it was on this account that . . . their place in Aldus' printing office was taken to a large extent by the sturdier and less sensitive letters . . . known as Poliphilus', i.e. the types which first appeared in the Aldine *Hypnerotomachia Poliphili* (1499). The Monotype recutting of these types, called Poliphilus, was first used for Morison's *Four Centuries of Fine Printing* (1924); and in 1926 in the Officina Bodoni edition, *Damianus Moyllus* (1927).

Mardersteig and Morison planned a book on Griffo's life and work which unfortunately was never published, as Morison died in 1967. In 1964, however, Mardersteig contributed an essay on Aldus Manutius and the letters of Francesco Griffo of Bologna to the three-volume studies in honour of Tammaro De Marinis.

81

a

PETRI BEMBI · DE AETNA LIBER
PIETRO BEMBO · ON ETNA

Latin text of the Aldine edition (1495), revised by Carlo Dionisotti, of the dialogue in which Pietro Bembo (later Cardinal Bembo) gives his father an account of his ascent of Mount Etna. With the first English translation, by Betty Radice. Postscript, including 'A Note on the types' by Giovanni Mardersteig. Dedicated to the memory of Stanley Morison. With a portrait of Bembo and facsimiles of an engraving of the villa 'Noniano' and of a page (f. A ii) of the Aldine edition.

125 copies printed on hand-made Cernobbio paper. Latin text set in 16-point Griffo roman, the English version in 16-point 'Monotype' Bembo roman and italic, and the Postscript in 12-point Bembo. 154 pages. 23.5×15.5 cm.
Editiones Officinae Bodoni: Verona, September 1969.
Dark pink Ingres paper boards with open device in gold on upper cover, red goatskin spine, top edge gilt, yellow and red headbands.
German and Italian editions were also issued.

This copy was printed for the British Museum.   Cup.510.ee.35

– Another copy.   *Ad personam.*   Loan

In 1493 Pietro Bembo, later Cardinal Bembo, climbed to the top of the volcano Etna in Sicily. On his return home to the villa Noniano near Padua he composed this Latin dialogue between himself and his father which gives the earliest detailed description of Etna.

b

Pietro BEMBO: *De Aetna*. Aldus Manutius: Venice, 1495.   G.9289

PETRI BEMBI
AD ANGELUM CHABRIELEM
DE AETNA LIBER.

Factum a nobis pueris est et quidem sedulo, Angele, quod meminisse te certo scio, ut fructus studiorum nostrorum, quos ferebat illa aetas non tam maturos quam uberes, semper tibi aliquos promeremus. Nam sive dolebas aliquid, sive gaudebas, quae duo sunt tenerorum animorum maxime propriae affectiones, continuo habebas aliquid a me', quod legeres, vel gratulationis, vel consolationis, imbecillum tu quidem illud et tenue, sicuti nascentia omnia et incipientia, sed tamen quod esset satis amplum futurum argumentum amoris summi erga te mei. Verum postea quam annis crescentibus et studia et iudicium increvere, nosque totos tradidimus graecis magistris erudiendos, remissiores paulatim facti sumus ad scribendum ac iam etiam minus quotidie audentiores.
II

fieri posse uix puto : sed plane quia ita debemus inter nos : neq; enim arbitror cariorem rem fuisse ulli quenquam ;q̃ tu sis mihi. Sed de his et diximus alias satis multa ; et saepe dicemus : nũc autem ; quoniam iam quotidie ferè accidit postea, q̃ e Sicilia ego, et tu reuersi sumus ; ut de Aetnae incendiis interrogaremus ab iis, quibus notum est illa nos satis diligenter perspexisse ; ut ea tandem molestia careremus; placuit mihi eum sermonem conscribere' ; quem cum Bernardo parente habui paucis post diebus, q̃ rediissemus ; ad quem reiiciendi essent ii , qui nos deinceps quippiam de Aetna postularent. Itaq; confeci librũ; quo uterq; nostrum cõmuniter uteretur : nã cum essemus in Noniano ; et pater se (ut solebat) ante atrium in ripam Pluuici contulisset; accessi ad eũ progresso iam in meridianas horas die : ubi ea, quae locuti sum° inter nos, ferè ista fũt. Tibi uero nũc oratione utriusq; nostrũ, tanq̃ habeatur,
A ii

Bembo, *De Aetna* (1969). Preface, set in Griffo and facsimile of a page of the 1495 edition. (81)

78

82

LO ALPHABETO DELLI VILLANI

A popular poem in the dialect of Venice and Vicenza of the year 1524, with Italian version by Emilio Lovarini and a postscript by the printer.
55 copies printed in red and black on hand-made Magnani paper.
Text set in 16-point Griffo italic, Italian version in 11-point Bembo, and the postscript in 13-point Bembo. 26 pages. 24.5×17 cm.
Private edition printed for the wedding of Alberto Falck and Cecilia Collato Giustiniani Recanati, 18 June 1969. Officina Bodoni: Verona, autumn 1969.
Brown and blue Castellare paper boards, vellum spine, top edge yellow, red headbands.   Loan

83

HUGH MACDIARMID
A DRUNK MAN LOOKS AT THE THISTLE

English text of poem, with notes and glossary by the author. Illustrated with woodcuts by Frans Masereel. All copies signed by the author, the artist and the printer.
160 copies printed on Amalfi paper hand-made by L. Amatruda.
Text set in 13-point Dante roman and italic, notes and glossary in 10-point.
148 pages. 29×19.5 cm.
Printed for Kulgin Duval & Colin Hamilton: Falkland, Fife, 1970. Verona, November 1969.
Blue on cream patterned Castellare paper boards, vellum spine with gilt line, top edge gilt, blue headbands.   Copy No. 5.   Cup.510.ee.32

– Another copy.   Copy No. 38.   Loan

84

IPPOLITO E LIONORA
From a Manuscript of Felice Feliciano in the Harvard College Library.

Italian text of the *novella* sometimes attributed to Leon Battista Alberti, transcribed by Franco Riva from the manuscript in the Harvard College Library, MS. Typ. 24, written by Felice Feliciano. With textual notes by Franco Riva and an English translation and a bibliography by Martin Faigel. Facsimiles of the manuscript and of a coloured initial N reproduced in offset by the Stamperia Valdonega. Preface by Philip Hofer. Essay 'On Felice Feliciano' by G. Mardersteig.

200 copies printed in red and black on hand-made Cernobbio paper.
Novella set in 12-point Dante roman. Preface set in 13-point Dante italic, notes
and essay in 11- and 8-point Dante. 120 pages. 24×16 cm.
Printed for the Department of Printing & Graphic Arts, Houghton Library,
Harvard College, Cambridge, Mass. Verona, February 1970.
Vellum-coloured Linson boards, top edge gilt, red headbands. Copy No. 54. Loan

– Another copy.   Copy No. 65. Loan

Ippolito e Lionora was a commission from the Department of Printing and Graphic
Arts at the Houghton Library, Harvard, who owned a manuscript written by Feliciano.
They decided to reproduce one of the tales in it in facsimile (undertaken by Marder-
steig's son Martino at the Stamperia Valdonega) with a transcript and English trans-
lation of the text, together with a note on Feliciano by Mardersteig printed at the
Officina Bodoni.

85

THE ALPHABET OF FRANCESCO TORNIELLO DA NOVARA
(1517) · *Followed by a comparison with the Alphabet of Fra Luca Pacioli.*
Introduction by Giovanni Mardersteig.

The original Italian text of a treatise by Torniello, 'On the method of forming
antique capital letters'. English translation by Betty Radice. The title-page woodcut
(a portrait of Torniello), recut by Italo Zetti; the geometric constructions of the
letters recut by Leonardo Farina. By way of individual comparison each letter of
Torniello's alphabet is then reproduced on the same page with the corresponding
letter of Luca de Pacioli's alphabet.
160 copies printed in black and blue on hand-made Amalfi paper by F. Amatruda.
Text set in 13- and 12-point Dante roman and italic. Translation in 11-point Dante
roman and italic. xxviii+106 pages. 27×19 cm.
Editiones Officinae Bodoni: Verona, January 1971.
Vellum-coloured Linson boards with FRANCESCO TORNIELLO, in Torniello's
alphabet reduced and printed in black, on upper cover and DA NOVARA on lower
cover, blue goatskin spine, top edge gilt, white headbands.
                                        Copy No. 147. Cup.510.ee.44

– Another copy.   *Ad personam.* Loan

The alphabet of Francesco Torniello of Novara, based mainly on Pacioli's roman
alphabet (1509), was printed in 1517 by Gotardo da Ponte in Milan in a writing-book
which has survived in only four copies. The introduction to the Officina Bodoni
edition deals with those who collaborated on the original edition: Torniello, the

author; Guillaume Le Signerre who cut the portrait of the author, the decorated initial and probably the woodblocks of the letters; and Da Ponte, the printer and publisher. It also gives a brief account of different alphabetic constructions up to 1529.

Torniello introduced a system of measurement based on the proportion which Pacioli used between the thickness of the stem (or principal stroke) and the height of the square grid on which his letters are constructed, i.e. 1:9. Torniello's is the first construction based on this rational measurement, which he called a 'point' and which corresponds to the thickness of the principal stroke or the ninth part of the height of a letter. In this way Pacioli's system gains much in precision and becomes more comprehensible.

Another typographical term was used for the first time by Torniello in this book, the word 'grazia', or serif, to define the slender cross-strokes at the head or foot of a letter.

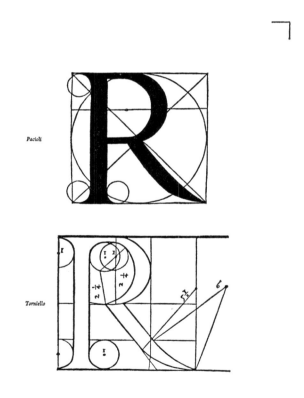

Pacioli

Torniello

86

a

THE LITTLE PASSION BY ALBRECHT DÜRER · *With the poems of the first edition of 1511 by Benedictus Chelidonius Musophilus in Latin with English version.*

The Latin poems are placed opposite the thirty-six woodcuts of Dürer. These and the Man of Sorrows woodcut on the title-page of the edition of 1511 all re-engraved by Leonardo Farina. The Latin text and woodcuts are followed by an English prose translation by Robert Fitzgerald and an essay by Giovanni Mardersteig on the printing of Dürer's woodcuts and on Chelidonius.
140 copies on hand-made Magnani paper of Pescia. Set in 12- and 11-point Dante roman and italic. 218 pages. 23×15.5 cm.
Editiones Officinae Bodoni: Verona, September 1971.
Ingres paper boards with gold rule, and the device in gold on upper cover, brown pig-skin spine. Copy No. 63.   Cup.510.ee.34

– Another copy. *Ad personam.*   Loan

– Another copy. *Ad personam.*   Loan

Christus duobus ex suis discipulis apparet in Emmaus. Ode glyco-
nica, choriambica, trimetra.

De summo quoties Deo
Fit sermo, medium, palam
Ipsus, clamve locum tenet,
Ut veri cupidis boni
At prave gradientibus
Præsto sensibus obviet
Et cæli doceat viam,
Vel recte sapientibus
Motus augeat excitos.
Sic olim Cleophæ pius
Et Lucæ Dominus parem
Se finxit comitem viæ:
Quos erroris ab invio
Verbi dogmate mystici
Veri duxit ad orbitam.
Ipsis tum, sub imagine
Convivæ, cererem manu
Ceu ferro penetrabili
Frangendo, patuit viris
Christus, panis olympicus.

b

Albrecht DÜRER: *Passio Christi*. (The Little Passion.) Nuremberg, 1511
Department of Prints and Drawings, British Museum. 1896-1-25-1 (1–37).

In the prints of Dürer's woodcuts from the few surviving copies of the 1511 edition
the delicate cross-hatching and white dots have sometimes been obscured or coarsened
by uneven inking. In this, the Mitchell copy, however, some of the impressions are
unusually fine.

c

Early impressions from the woodcuts by Albrecht Dürer for the *Little Passion*.
Nos. 17 and 20 are mounted with nos. 18 and 19.
Department of Prints and Drawings, British Museum. E.2-223–226, 233, 235, 236, 237.

These impressions taken before the publication of the 1511 volume are remarkably
clean and accurate.

d

Albrecht DÜRER: Two of the original woodblocks for *The Little Passion*:
1 Adam and Eve eating the fruit of the Tree of Life. B.VII, p. 119, no. 17.
2 The Nativity. B.VII, p. 120, no. 20.
Department of Prints and Drawings, British Museum. 1839-6-8-3.

In 1511 Dürer published in book form three of his great series of woodcuts on religious
subjects. The Great Passion, the Life of the Virgin, and, so called from its smaller
format, the Little Passion. In each volume the woodcuts received the addition of a
Latin text to face Dürer's woodcuts, evidently commissioned by Dürer himself
from the monk and humanist Benedictus Chelidonius, whose real name was Benedikt
Schwalbe. He took care that in each poem the number of lines should not exceed
the height of the facing woodcut.

Dürer drew the design for his illustrations on the woodblock; the design was then
cut on the block usually by a craftsman, the *Formschneider*. Thus the finished woodcuts depend for their effect on the eye and hand of a collaborator who transposed the
pen drawing into engraving technique, under Dürer's supervision. Moreover, the
contemporary practice of inking the blocks with ink-balls did not distribute the ink
as evenly on the surface as the modern roller does, so that some blocks, after many
printings, became dirty and blackened. For the Officina Bodoni edition it was decided
that, instead of using retouched photographic reproductions of the original impressions, new blocks from wood should be cut by a modern craftsman, Leonardo
Farina.

87

a

A COMEDY OF TERENCE CALLED ANDRIA

Translated into English by Richard Bernard with twenty-five illustrations by Albrecht Dürer.

English text by Richard Bernard (1598), revised and edited by Betty Radice.
Illustrated with 25 woodcuts by Fritz Kredel after the drawings made by Albrecht Dürer on blocks now in the Kunstmuseum, Basel: 24 scenes from the comedy and a frontispiece showing Terence writing.
Postscript by Giovanni Mardersteig on the young Dürer in Basel and on contemporary illustrated editions of Terence.
160 numbered copies and ten copies *ad personam* printed on hand-made Magnani paper. Text set in 14-point Dante roman and italic; postscript and notes in 13-point Dante roman and italic.
126 pages. 35×25 cm.
Editiones Officinae Bodoni: Verona, November 1971.
Yellow Fabriano Roma paper boards with gold rule, and open device in gold on upper cover, vellum spine.   Printed for the British Museum.   c.127.k.11

This edition was also issued in a German text, a translation made at the age of sixteen by the composer Felix Mendelssohn and published in 1826, revised by Rudolf Hagelstange; and in an Italian text, the version of Machiavelli.

b

Albrecht Dürer: Illustrations to Terence's comedies drawn on woodblocks
(a volume of photographs of the blocks preserved in the Kupferstichkabinett, Kunstmuseum, Basel).

Department of Prints and Drawings, British Museum. 36*.a.10.

Dürer's illustrations for two of Terence's comedies, *Andria* and *Eunuchus*, were drawn by pen on woodblocks *c.* 1492, for an illustrated edition of Terence planned by the Basel printer Johann Amerbach. This edition was never published because it was anticipated by the Terence produced by Trechsel at Lyon in August 1493. Most of Dürer's drawings on the blocks were never cut and survive in Basel along with the blocks by other artists which illustrate the other Terence comedies.

On the reverse of the blocks the humanist Sebastian Brant provided rough sketches showing the disposition of the figures and indications of their names and the act and scene. Dürer's drawings show the characters, not in a theatre against the backcloth of a stage, but against contemporary street scenes. The young dandies Pamphilus and Charinus are especially attractive.

Fritz Kredel described his cutting of the Dürer designs in an article in *Philobiblon*, November 1971. In his own view, his task was to translate Dürer's drawings into the language of woodcuts in which they were originally intended to be expressed.

The freely-drawn pen drawings were obviously made without much preparatory sketching. In many instances it seems as if only a bare indication was given to the engraver, to whom Dürer allowed a relatively free hand, e.g. with walls, trees, bridges, bushes. Great skill, however, is shown in presentation of drapery and facial features. The backgrounds of streets and open squares reveal much about the appearance of a contemporary town, and the costumes and head gear are richly fantastic.

In the Officina Bodoni edition the drawings for *Andria*, re-engraved on pearwood blocks by Fritz Kredel, were published for the first time in Dürer's quincentenary year—in Mardersteig's words, 'as a late tribute'.

Woodcut designs by Dürer cut by Fritz Kredel for Terence, *Andria* (1971). (87)

88

In fair Verona · English travellers in Italy and their accounts of the city from the Middle Ages to Modern Times.
(Presented to Giovanni Mardersteig by his friends on his eightieth birthday, 8 January 1972.)   Cup.510.ac.39

Thirty-nine British and American friends of Mardersteig's produced this book as an eightieth birthday present.

The idea for this book and its subject came from Hans Schmoller. The passages were selected by Nicolas Barker, who also wrote the linking text. The whole was set in Dante at the Curwen Press, Plaistow. Reynolds Stone engraved the device on the title-page. One hundred copies were printed by Will and Sebastian Carter at the Rampant Lions Press and bound at the University Printing House, both in Cambridge.

Le Rime di Ser Garzo dall'Incisa (1972). First verse of *lauda* 'Altissima Luce'. (89)

89

LE RIME DI SER GARZO DALL'INCISA

The original Italian text edited and with a note by Ada Ronzini. The initials and
half-titles of the three parts of the volume are printed in different colours:
I Proverbi in blue; *La Leggenda di S. Caterina* in green; and *Cinque laude* in red, as are
the notes of music of the first *lauda*, 'Altissima Luce', transcribed by Carlo Magnani
from Codex Cortonese 91. The title-page and the three half-titles each have a
different typographical framework.
150 copies printed in black, red, blue and green on hand-made Magnani paper.
The main title-page printed in red 16- and 30-point Zeno. Text set in 14-point Zeno,
notes in 11-point Dante roman and italic.
130 pages. 24.5×16 cm.
Editiones Officinae Bodoni: Verona, May 1972.
Brown patterned Fabriano Ingres paper boards designed by Martino Mardersteig
and printed at the Stamperia Valdonega, tan buffalo leather spine with gilt line,
dark red leather label on spine, top edge gilt, red and yellow headbands.

Copy No. 148.   Cup.510.ee.36

– Another copy.

Copy No. 142.   Loan

The writings of Ser Garzo dall'Incisa, Petrarch's great-grandfather, are for the first
time collected in this edition. His *laude* were sung in church; their melodies survive
in various manuscripts and one is printed here. The colours used in the three parts
are found in thirteenth-century manuscripts.

90

EUGENIO MONTALE · IL POETA · DIARIO

Italian text of the poems.
165 copies printed in black and blue on hand-made Magnani paper. Colophon
signed by the poet.
Poems set in 18-point Dante italic, second state, other text in 12-point Dante roman
and italic.
62 pages. 30×20.5 cm.
Editiones Officinae Bodoni: Verona, November 1972.
Blue and black printed patterned paper boards, white vellum spine with gilt line,
blue headbands.

Copy No. 135.   Loan

91

THE FABLES OF AESOP. *Printed from the Veronese edition of 1479 in Latin verses and the Italian version by Accio Zucco, with the woodcuts newly engraved and coloured after a copy in the British Museum.*

The English edition consists of 160 copies, as follows:
30 sets in three volumes.
Vol. 1 contains the fables in Latin and Italian with 68 hand-coloured woodcuts and an epilogue. 282 pages.
Vol. 2 contains the fables in Caxton's translation without illustrations. 122 pages.
Vol. 3 contains the woodcuts in black and white without the text. 150 pages.
130 sets in two volumes, i.e. vols. 1 and 2.
Printed on Magnani hand-made paper with the watermark of the goose reproduced from the original edition. Set in 16- and 12-point Centaur; initials in 13-point Centaur.
25×16.5 cm. Editiones Officinae Bodoni: Verona, February–March 1973.
White vellum covers with interlacing fillets and Alvise flower and title in gold, green goatskin spine, top edge gilt, green and yellow headbands.

No. 1. Printed for the British Museum.   c.131.ff.1

a

Vol. 1. Text of the Fables in anonymous Latin elegiacs; each fable followed by a *sonetto materiale* and a *sonetto morale* in Italian by Accio Zucco from Sommacampagna, near Verona; both texts revised by G. B. Pighi. Epilogue, in English, by Giovanni Mardersteig on Aesop, on the Verona Aesop edition of 1479 and its illustrator, and on other fifteenth-century Italian illustrated editions of Aesop.
68 woodcuts attributed to Liberale da Verona recut by Anna Bramanti, hand-coloured in Paris by the Atelier Daniel Jacomet after the British Library copy
c.1.a.5.   Copy No. 1.   c.131.ff.1

– Another copy.   *Ad personam.*   Loan

– Another copy.   *Ad personam.*   Copy No. 2.   Loan

b

AESOP: *Fables.* Giovanni Alvise: Verona, 1479.   c.1.a.5

c

Vol. 2 The first three books of Caxton's Aesop, containing the fables illustrated in the Verona Aesopus of 1479.

English text of sixty fables in William Caxton's version, first published in 1484. The first fable and the final six of the Verona edition which Caxton did not include are translated by Betty Radice. Introductory note, revision, punctuation and modernized spelling by Tanya and Hans Schmoller.
Binding as for Vol. 1, with the title CAXTON'S AESOP WESTMINSTER 1484 in gold on the spine and CAXTON'S AESOP in gold on the upper cover.

Copy No. 1.   c.131.ff.5(2)

d

Vol. 3 The woodcuts engraved for the Fables of the Veronese Aesop of 1479 and recut for this edition in black and white by Anna Bramanti.

Binding as for Vol. 1, with the title AESOP WOODCUTS IN BLACK AND WHITE in gold on the spine and AESOPUS on the upper cover.   Copy No. 1.   c.131.ff.5(3)

– Another copy.

Ad personam.   Copy No. 2.   Loan

DE MURE RUSTICO ET URBANO
.F. XIII

DE LUPO ET GRUE
.F. VIIII

Mardersteig marked the fiftieth anniversary of the Officina Bodoni by the publication of the *Fables* of Aesop, his reinterpretation of a fine illustrated book printed in Verona in 1479 by Giovanni Alvise. Alvise, the third printer in Verona (active 1478–80), was also the first printer to use typographical ornaments cast in lead as separate characters. They were modelled on contemporary manuscript decoration. Mardersteig had Alvise's ornaments recut by Charles Malin and used them in several books, including this one, where the woodcuts are surrounded by borders of printers' flowers, as in the 1479 Aesop.

For the Officina Bodoni edition the original woodcuts were also recut by a contemporary engraver and coloured by hand. Mardersteig took as a model for the colouring one of the three copies of the Verona Aesop in the British Museum (now the British Library) which is by far the finest of the four surviving coloured copies. They are not coloured in the usual primitive fashion of fifteenth-century woodcuts, i.e. in a few strong colours without subtle shading. The excellence of the colouring suggested to Mardersteig the work of an artist who evidently visualized the cuts and their colouring as a unity, and was probably himself the designer of the cuts.

The Aesop cuts show a rich spectrum of colours with delicate hues that recall miniatures. Mardersteig maintained that only a great master could have made the preliminary drawings for the fable illustrations and had in mind at the outset the colouring which would give life to the linear woodcuts. This artist he identified on stylistic grounds with the miniaturist Liberale da Verona, whose paintings are to be seen in the large choir-books in the Piccolomini Library in Siena Cathedral and elsewhere.

92

G. Mardersteig: *Liberale ritrovato nell'Esopo Veronese del 1479 . . . con una nota introduttiva di Licisco Magagnato.* Museo di Castelvecchio: Verona, 1973.
Printed by the Stamperia Valdonega.

Mardersteig's epilogue to his Aesop edition was here reprinted to accompany an exhibition of the work of Liberale da Verona.   x.410/5277

93

SONGS FROM SHAKESPEARE'S PLAYS

English text edited with a postscript by Brian Deakin. Shakespeare's 'The
Phoenix and Turtle' is included at the request of the printer in an appendix,
in the text and spelling of the first printing of 1601.
310 copies: 10 *ad personam* on vellum and 300 on hand-made Pescia paper. Set in
14- and 12-point Dante italic, slightly modified. Italic initials and arabesques in red.
50 pages. 27 × 17.5 cm.
Editiones Officinae Bodoni: Verona, March 1974.
Green and white woven fabric, patterned with animals and birds, green goatskin
spine with gilt line, top edge gilt, yellow headbands.   Copy No. 55.   Cup.510.ee.42

– Another copy.   Copy No. 5.   Loan

SONGS
from
SHAKESPEARE'S
PLAYS

MDCCCCLXXIIII

VERONA

A LETTER
FROM
THE REVEREND MASTER
BERNARDINO OF FLORENCE, FORMER-
LY PREACHER IN THE CHURCH OF SAN
FERMO, IN PRAISE OF THE COMMUNITY
OF VERONA, TO THE DISTINGUISHED
CITIZEN OF FLORENCE
GIOVANNI NESI.

SALUTATIONS TO YOU,
best of friends! I made up my mind a long time
ago, from the moment I left you in Florence,
that some day I would write you a letter of sin-
cere gratitude for your particular kindness to me,
which I well know, and at the same time would
send you my greetings. But I kept putting this off,
being prevented by my pressing duty to deliver
speeches, or rather sermons; and besides, I could
not think what to write which would give pleasure
to us both. But now that I am relieved of my
preaching obligations and have a little free time
on my hands, I will carry out my earlier resolution

29

94

BERNARDINO BARDUZZI
A LETTER IN PRAISE OF VERONA (1489)
*The original Latin text of 1489 edited by G. B. Pighi, with an English translation by
Betty Radice.*

Decorated with a large initial and half-titles in black, red, blue and yellow after
manuscripts by the fifteenth-century Veronese calligrapher and antiquary Felice
Feliciano, together with a drawing of an inscription by him. Postscript in English
by Giovanni Mardersteig.
150 copies printed in black, red and blue on hand-made Magnani paper of Pescia.
Set in 13-point Dante roman and 12-point Dante roman and italic.
58 pages. 25 × 16.5 cm.
Editiones Officinae Bodoni: Verona, December 1974.
Blue patterned Roma Fabriano paper covers, vellum spine with gilt line, top
edge gilt, blue headbands.
                              Copy No. 67.   Cup.403.p.19

Bernardino Barduzzi (d. 1497), a Florentine theologian and preacher of the Franciscan Order, was invited to preach in Verona, where he stayed several months in order to study the ancient Roman remains. His letter to his brother Franciscan, Joannes Nesi, a member of Marsilio Ficino's Florentine Platonic Academy, about his sojourn in Verona is one of the rare descriptions from the fifteenth century of an Italian town. The letter was printed in Verona in May 1489 by Paulus Fridenperger.

The original edition, of which only two copies survive, has no ornament; the decorations used in the Officina Bodoni edition were copied from manuscripts written and illuminated between 1460 and 1465 by Felice Feliciano.

95

NIKOLAY GOGOL · THE OVERCOAT · *From the Tales of Petersburg*

Original Russian text with English translation by Constance Garnett. Six etchings by Pietro Annigoni. After the text a note by the printer. The colophon signed by the artist.
160 copies printed in black and green on hand-made Magnani paper. The Russian text is set in 14-point Puškin, the Cyrillic face designed by Wadim Lazursky; the English translation in 14-point Dante, and notes in 13-point Dante. Half-title and initials in shadowed Puškin and Dante titling.
126 pages. 30×20.5 cm.
Editiones Officinae Bodoni: Verona, May 1975.
Light brown Roma Fabriano paper covers with solid device in gold on upper cover, vellum spine with gilt line, light brown paper label, top edge gilt, green and yellow headbands.
Copy No. 58. Cup.407.a.87

This edition was also published with an Italian translation.

The Russian text is set in the Cyrillic letter cut specially for the Officina Bodoni to harmonize with the Dante type and first used to print Pushkin's poem *Il Cavaliere di bronzo* (1968). The setting of a page of this prose text is, however, on average two lines longer in Cyrillic than the same text set in English or Italian, and so the arrangement of the Russian text and the translation on facing pages was abandoned. The unusual typographical solution in the present edition, i.e. printing both texts on one page, was made possible by the harmony of the Puškin and Dante type faces.

Gogol was living in the Via Sistina in Rome between 1838 and 1842 when he wrote *Dead Souls* and the first draft of *The Overcoat*.

96

a

ΔΕΛΦΙΚΑ ΓΡΑΜΜΑΤΑ
THE SAYINGS OF THE SEVEN SAGES OF GREECE

Greek text, based mainly on the version of Joannes Stobaeus, with an English translation by Betty Radice. Postscript by Giovanni Mardersteig on the history of the text and on the development of Greek letter-forms.
160 copies printed in black and terracotta on Magnani hand-made paper.
The Greek text of the Sayings set in 16-point Griffo Greek capitals; the English translation in 16-point Griffo roman, and the Postscript in 13-point Griffo roman.
The Delphic inscriptions and the names of the Sages on the half-titles are printed on a terracotta ground in black Greek block letters derived from an Athenian inscription of 408–407 BC.
90 pages. 25×16.5 cm.
Editiones Officinae Bodoni: Verona, April 1976.
Grey Ingres paper boards with a geometric decoration in terracotta, vellum spine with gilt line. Copy No. 150.   x.981/11109

– Another copy. *Ad personam.*   Loan

The Sayings of the Seven Sages of Greece belong to the beginnings of pre-Socratic philosophy. According to tradition, each of these wise men dedicated one of his maxims to Apollo and the seven Delphic maxims were inscribed on his temple at Delphi. In the Officina Bodoni edition the Greek text is translated into English, apparently for the first time, by Betty Radice.

The seven Delphic maxims are printed in black capitals on a terracotta background. The letters for these and for the half-titles were copied from an inscription on marble of 408–407 BC in honour of Oeniades of Palaiskiathos (Athens Epigraphic Museum, no. 6796). Mardersteig relates that when he was copying the exact size and proportions of the characters in this inscription he noticed that while most letters have an average height of 10 mm, the round letters and 'x' are only 7–8 mm high. 'Possibly the different heights of the letters would make them easier to read, by being less tiring for the eye', he suggests. He also observes that whereas in Greek inscriptions of the fifth century BC the letters rarely exceed 10 mm in height, in Roman incised inscriptions the letters were larger so that they could be read from a distance. 'Later on, under the influence and domination of Rome, the Greek characters . . . were made to conform with Latin capital letters where the height is the same throughout the alphabet'.

The Greek text of the Sayings is printed in Greek capitals based on those cut in 1494 by the goldsmith and punch-cutter Francesco Griffo for the first works published by Aldus Manutius, at about the same time as he cut the roman types in which

Aldus printed Pietro Bembo's *De Aetna*. 'The Greek and Latin capitals complemented each other and were matched in perfect harmony', Mardersteig continues: 'Forty years later in Paris, Claude Garamond copied several alphabets designed by Griffo, amongst them the roman type of the *De Aetna* and the Greek capitals'. As we have seen, in 1929–30 the roman alphabet used in Bembo's book was recut for the Officina Bodoni by Charles Malin. 'A decade later he also cut the eleven Greek letters in the style perfected by Garamond. The happy combination of Greek and Latin capitals appears again in this publication'.

b

Fragment of a marble stele recording a decree appointing a commission to resume building operations on the unfinished Erechtheum, 409 BC.

(Photograph of BM Inscription 7, Elgin Collection.)

In this inscription, contemporary with the one studied by Mardersteig, the letters show the same variations in height, i.e. those of circular shape are 8 mm high, the alphas and deltas are 10 mm and some of the letters starting with a vertical stroke up to 15 mm in height. In a *stoichedon* inscription like this (where the letters are aligned in columns as well as in rows) the widths of the letters are at least as important as their heights. It could well be that this deliberate variation in letter sizes occurs primarily for aesthetic reasons.

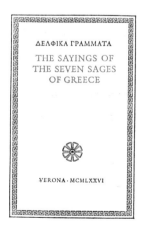

ΔΕΛΦΙΚΑ ΓΡΑΜΜΑΤΑ

THE SAYINGS OF
THE SEVEN SAGES
OF GREECE

VERONA · MCMLXXVI

97

ERO E LEANDRO · *Una leggenda greca di Museo.*

Italian verse translation with notes by Enzio Centrangolo of the Greek epyllion by
Musaeus (*fl.* 4th–5th century AD): the tale in verse of the tragic love of Hero and
Leander. Etchings by Enrico Paulucci. Signed by the artist.
112 copies printed in black and blue: 12 *ad personam* copies on Japanese Kaji
Torinoko paper and 100 copies on hand-made Cernobbio paper. 28.5×20 cm.
Text set in 14-point Dante roman, notes in 12-point Dante roman and italic.
Private edition, Novara 1977. Officina Bodoni: Verona, January 1977.
Blue and dark grey Cockerell marbled paper boards, royal blue goatskin spine,
gold line, top edge gilt, green, red and yellow headbands.   Copy No. 53.   Loan

98

Auguri cards.

A selection of cards conveying greetings, mainly for the New Year, from the
printer to his friends. On these cards Mardersteig often used designs, types and
illustrations in advance of their appearance in Officina Bodoni books.   Loan

Auguri card (1964) with woodcut rebus from the *Polifilo* of Aldus Manutius. (98)